喚醒你的英文語感 ！

Get a Feel for English !

喚醒你的英文語感！

Get a Feel for English !

得心應手寫英文

迎戰

高分寫作

適用各項英文考試

TOEIC × TOEFL
IELTS × GRE
GMAT × 公職特考
研究所 × 學士後中西醫

Idea
Organization
Word choice
Sentence
structure

4大寫作基本能力

| 批判思考 | 邏輯呈現 | 遣詞用字 | 文法句型 |

穩紮穩打
一氣呵成！

作者／登峰名師 **文喬**

審閱／Quentin Brand

貝塔語言出版
Beta Multimedia Publishing

登峰美語系列

　　只要討論到「英文能力檢定」類型的考試，大家通常會直接想到考聽力、文法、閱讀文章那些傳統考題。若背背文法規則或瞭解解題技巧，可能還會得到不錯的成績。但若說到「英文寫作」部份，可以說是八成以上同學的夢魘！第一句就無法下筆了不說，還會遭遇到：想不出要寫什麼點子／內容，中式英文句子，遣詞用字很侷限，寫出來的句型仍停留在初級簡單句的階段……等嚴重問題。

　　現實點說，英文寫作可以說是一面可以反映出個人英語方面在「思考邏輯」，「文法句型」，與「單字運用」的照妖鏡。寫出的文章層次到哪，馬上會讓一個人英語程度無所遁形！雖說英文寫作能力並非一朝一夕就可養成的，但針對市場上各類制式化的英文寫作考試來說，還是可以歸納出一些寫作要點，讓同學有機可循，進而書寫出較像樣的文章／內容，藉以提高分數的。

　　有鑑於此，筆者便針對托福、雅思、研究所、公職特考、學士後中西醫、多益等常考的各類寫作題材，幫同學整理快速可以利用的寫作要點，包括：寫作前的準備功課，各種詞性單字的同義字拓展，實用句型的歸納，文章整體架構的建立，與思考點子的方式等。 除了能協助同學從「不知如何下筆」提升到「可以寫出結構完整，內容清楚的文章」之外，長遠地來看，更期望同學可以藉由準備的過程中，透過背單字，學句型等努力，進而提升自身整體的英文程度。以期日後不管遇到何種類型的英文寫作需求（例如：英文寫作考試、寫報告、公司寫 email、求職用英文自傳等），都可以更加地得心應手。

文喬

CONTENTS

CHAPTER 1／提升基礎能力

UNIT 1：遣詞用字

UNIT 2：文法句型

CHAPTER 2 ／ 正式寫作

UNIT 3：掌握寫作結構

UNIT 4：實務寫作——綜合範文 10 篇

UNIT 5：點子發想有方向

附錄

應試作文會診

打造完整 Essay 寫作能力，從容應對各項考試的寫作題

　　不論是何種「目的」的考試（留學，公職，升學等），也不管是何種「類型」的英文能力檢定（TOEIC，TOEFL，會考，研究所等），除了基本的聽力與閱讀能力測驗外，口語的表達與英文作文的書寫更是必考題型。

　　在台灣，同學若有需要使用口語的機會，還可能靠講講簡易的單字外加表情或比手劃腳，要求能溝通，對方聽得懂意思就好。但是，「英文寫作」這任務可就沒這麼好過關了，也因此「英文寫作」成為多數備考同學的夢魘，看到一個議題就腦筋一片空白完全沒概念，更別說「連第一句要寫什麼都想不出來的」窘境了。為了協助同學解決寫作問題，提供寫作方向，更為了培養扎實的英文實力，遂有了本書的誕生。

　　雖說各式不同英文能力測驗的考試，寫作題型各有出入（如：TOEIC 有考寫 email，或 TOEFL iBT 有考 Integrated 整合寫作……等），幾乎每種英檢寫作題都會有的題型就是闡述論點，表達自己看法的 Essay 題。本書內容會將焦點放在 Essay 題的寫作教戰上，以期協助同學可以在平均 30 分鐘的考試時間內，有能力寫到 300 字以上，且言之有物的英文文章。

☆ 各種題型
獨立寫作、意見論文、email……

☆ 各種考試
TOEIC、TOEFL、IELTS、公職特考、研究所、升學、英檢

☆ 應考時間／文章長度
20-40 分鐘不等
220~350 字左右

↓

都能以闡述論點、表達看法的
Essay 論述文寫作
應戰

實力養成

如何在平日做好英文寫作的實力培養？

首先，若您抱著「看完本書，寫作自然文思泉湧」的期待來學習的話，那麼筆者要先建議您改變一下心態。要知道，「英文寫作」能力，可以說是靠相當長期的、各種思考／文字方面能力的累積，包括：

1. (Idea) 批判思考能力

是否有精闢獨到的見解，意見具說服力，讓人過目不忘。

2. (Organization) 邏輯呈現方式

整體的意見呈現方式，是否讓讀者易於瞭解，文中內容起承轉合是否順暢。

3. (Word choice) 遣詞用字程度

所使用的單字是否符合程度，並且精準又恰當。

4. (Sentence structure) 文法句型變化

寫出的句子是否跳脫僅能寫簡單句的框框，進而可運用各種句型（比方說：倒裝句，關係子句等），讓讀者可完全瞭解意涵。

而這四個基本能力，要有個人化的點子，邏輯概念，用字精準，還要運用文法句型變化能力，其中沒有一個是可以一蹴可及，想要靠什麼「速效」，「神蹟」，或「猜題」等奇怪的英文學習方式就足以達成的。這四個最基礎能力，除了靠穩紮穩打，透過不斷閱讀英文文章，收集資訊，徹底瞭解單字用法，依實用句型來造句之外，實在是沒有其他辦法可以讓「英文寫作」精進的。因此，除了參考本書內的寫作建議之外，請考生務必在日常生活中確切地做好實力培養的準備：

➊ 點子的收集來源

要寫會得高分的文章，絕對不可能是靠 templates 寫作模板，和隨處找來的英文用語試圖拼拼湊湊、疊床架屋就可以過關的。若文章空有其表，內容卻了無新意，看不出您要表達的點子和別人的有何差異之處，讓人過目即忘，還是無法取得理想分數的。文章內點子與內涵的重要性自然不在話下，因此，同學平時就應該透過多觀察和多閱讀來收集點子，同時透過參考他人不同意見，來培養批判思考、從別的角度看事情的能力。平時可以靠以下幾種方式收集到可寫的點子或看法：

☑ **個人的經驗**：既然是自己親身體驗過的，不是強記模板內容，自然是最好發揮。建議同學多利用跟自身相關的實例。

☑ **對他人的觀察所得之看法**：即便不是自己親身經歷過的事，我們也常由周遭親朋好友處得到資訊。這些由他人處看到或聽到的真實事例，也可當例子。

☑ **個人獨到的看法**：但較為偏頗的看法考官不一定贊同，故使用上要謹慎。例如，社會正提倡不要吸煙，可是偏偏你個人的看法是 Smoking is good ... 這樣可能比較危險一點。

☑ **自書籍得知的知識**：可能是看了 *The Grapes of the Wrath* 的心得，或閱讀了 *The Wind in the Willows* 的感想等，都對增加文章可看性有幫助。

☑ **數據／歷史／名人提過的智慧之語**：這些確切發生過的事，來當例證是最具說服力的了。有數據，實際事件，或甚至 Steve Jobs 所講過的話，都可以讓論點更具可看性。

☑ **報章雜誌／論文**：很多知名的權威雜誌，像是 TIME，Success Magazine，或甚至於 The Economist 等雜誌所寫的內容，都具不同切入角度，值得參考。

☑ **演講或網路**……等

尤其，現今社會中資訊如此發達，對自身內涵與知識的收集與建立可以說是 no excuse，沒有藉口可以說做不到的。因此，請同學在準備寫好「英文作文」之前，一定要培養收集資料，獨立思考，和發展看法點子的能力。

❷ 力求文法正確，提升句子精鍊度

在筆者十數年的英文教學期間，根據修改過數千篇的英文作文的經驗，發現普遍台灣同學（尤其是大學生）的英文文法概念都頗薄弱。所寫出的句子通常會有：冗長乏味，文法錯誤，一句內出現數個動詞，句子僅是文字組合，再隨意以逗號隔開而已，連個連接詞都沒有……等嚴重文法問題。這樣的寫作方式不但無法讓讀者瞭解文句意思，也會被視為有重大文法錯誤而被扣分。

就算有些同學的基本文法概念沒問題，但也僅能以「簡單句」的方式傳達意思，而沒有將句子精進美化的能力，導致句子看來就是停留在「兒童美語」的程度。比方說 I don't want to do the job. 此句文法是沒錯，但還是可以運用片語 be reluctant to 來修改為 I'm reluctant to take on the responsibility.。由此可以看出，寫英文作文不應停留在「有寫就好」的期待。而更應該要有運用單字、片語與句型等能力，力求句子的簡潔與美化。

因此，要精進英文寫作程度之前，同學務必先將最基本的文法概念做一番徹底的複習與瞭解，比方像：主詞動詞一致、平行結構、單複數概念、比較結構、關係子句……等，這些文法概念都可以參考 Azar-Hagen Grammar Series 那三本文法書的解釋與練習。另外，其他實用的可以讓同學馬上套用的寫作句型會另外在 unit 2 章節中討論。

❸ 遣詞用字

單字的運用也是讓讀者看出考生英文寫作程度的環節。若文中僅使用兩三千個字量的初級單字，便僅能表達出很初步的意思，無法將句子的質感提升的。很多同學誤以為遣詞用字程度要提升，就一定是不能寫簡單的字，非得用超難 GRE 等級的字不可。這種觀念也是不必要的。

單字的運用不在於單字本身的難易度，重點是考生在運用單字時，可否精確地傳達到自己的意思。比方說此句內 He is a very good speaker. 的形容詞 good 偏向初級單字，且句意「他是位很好的講者。」會讓讀者有「很好是多好呢？」的疑惑。此句若換個形容詞 articulate「能言善道，說話清楚的」使用，改為 He is a very articulate speaker. 便可傳達出「他是一個表達無礙，讓人一聽就懂」的演講者。由此例子可看

出，單字的運用會影響到句子的明確度，在寫作上實爲相當重要的一環。（更多初級單字與常用的寫作替換字，在 unit 1 章節會以表格方式清楚地列出。）

那麼，同學要養成記單字的習慣。此處所說的「記單字」不僅僅是「背拼法」和「瞭解中文意思」就足夠的喔！而是除了可以拼得出來，和瞭解中文意思之外，還要徹底瞭解一個單字的：

◇ **詞性**：此單字是否有名詞形，動詞形，形容詞，副詞⋯⋯等。

◇ **片語**：此單字是否有其他片語，慣用語之用法。

◇ **同義字**：學一單字時，至少要順便記下其另外三個同義字，以便日後寫作可替換運用。（比方說 articulate 一字另有 expressive、persuasive、與 fluent 等同義字。）這類同義字的拓展，可準備一本「牛津英語同義詞學習詞典／Oxford Learner's Thesaurus」來隨時參考。

◇ **反義字**：若可一併將反義字也記下，更可提升對單字的瞭解。（比方說 articulate 的反義字有 unclear，tongue-tied 等。）

◇ **搭配字**：有時寫作時會詞窮，一部份是因爲不瞭解單字還可以如何與其他字搭配之故。若可以進一步學習單字的「搭配字」，在拓展單字量和深入瞭解單字用法上，將更如虎添翼。比方說，大家熟知的 knowledge 一字，通常就會使用 learn 來與之搭配，形成 learn knowledge（學習知識）。但若可以運用其他的搭配字的話，還會有 gain knowledge、acquire knowledge、obtain knowledge 或甚至 expand the scope of knowledge 等遣詞用字的變化就多樣化了起來，不是嗎？這類的「搭配字」單字學習工具書，較知名的就是「牛津英語搭配詞典／Oxford Collocation Dictionary」，同學可以在一般大書局內找到。（牛津英文字典線上版：http://www.oxforddictionaries.com/）

討論到單字片語，此處便一併討論一下慣用語 (idiomatic expressions) 的使用。有時同學會覺得寫作時僅使用簡單句會詞不達意，可以試著使用慣用語來更貼切地表達。比方說，想表達「我不知我該往哪方向去」的意思，台灣同學很有可能就直接翻成 I don't know what to do in the future. 了。但若使用慣用語 be at the crossroads 將整

句改爲 I'm at the crossroads in my life. 的話，句子瞬間由台式英文句子變身爲道地的自然英文句子了。

「我不知我該往哪方向去。」的英語表達：	
中文思考 I don't know what to do in the future.	**自然英語** I'm at the crossroads in my life.

另一個例子是，有同學寫「塞翁失馬，焉知非福」的意思，便直接中譯爲 "A man called Simon lost his horse …"，這樣的句子會讓老外摸不著頭緒，更別提他們會知道 Simon 是誰了！殊不知，此句的意思可由慣用語 a blessing in disguise 來表達，例句："Losing my job turned out to be a blessing in disguise; I never would have found this new job if it hadn't happened." 「丟了工作焉知不是壞事呢」（若沒失去上個工作，我也不可能找到這個新工作呀！）由此可見，idiomatic expressions 的運用影響也是相當深遠的。

但是，筆者要鄭重地強調，可以自然地使用慣用語的前提是，考生必須徹底地瞭解一個慣用語的意義、使用時機等。絕對不要在對慣用語一知半解的情況下冒然地使用，恐怕會造成言不及意，或讓人誤解的情況。有興趣瞭解更多 idioms 與其意思／用法，可參考網站：http：//www.idiomsite.com/

以上所討論到的「點子／意見的收集」，「基本文法概念的建立」，與「對單字用法的徹底瞭解」這些基本工夫，都要靠同學在日常的學習與累積。這些基礎都穩固地具備之後，再來參考書內的寫作建議才會有事半功倍的效果。

Chapter 1

提升基礎能力

UNIT 1 ▶ 遣詞用字

　　相信許多同學都有相同的心聲：自小在學校上課開始，英文也學了一、二十年了，但寫起英文作文來還是脫離不了中式語感，遣詞用字也一直停留在初級用字的程度，始終用不出高層次的單字，也無法使用道地的英文表示法。的確，不管學多久的英文，因受到母語（中文）的影響，台灣同學在寫文章（或口說）方面還是有傾向以中文思考的方式來呈現英文意思。比方說，要表達「那間超市離我家很近。」之意，依照中文思考的話，這樣的句子 The supermarket is very near my home. 很可能就脫口而出了，而不會以自然的方式 That supermarket is just within walking distance. 來表示。

「那間超市離我家很近。」的英語表達：	
中文思考 The supermarket is very near my home.	自然英語 That supermarket is just within walking distance.

　　會有這樣的結果，若把原因都推給「受到中文干擾」，便感覺到束手無策的話，未免也太被動消極！事實上，要一點一滴地扭轉我們的「中式思考方式」也是可以靠積極的方式策略來達成的，例如：多聽自然英文對話，多閱讀英文文章，有意識地使用英文句型來寫句子，和多使用英文單字之同義字等。其中，最基本要做到紮實的功夫便是「單字量」的擴展了。若同學單字量有限，都只停留在 3000-4000 字的簡單單字，寫作時便難以表達較複雜的意思。

一、遣詞用字的改善方法

要改善這樣的用字問題，筆者提供三個方式給同學參考：

❶ 以「背同義字」來擴充單字量

比方說：

✓ free	→	**complimentary**（免費的）
✓ rich	→	**wealthy**（富有的）
✓ growth	→	**prosperity**（繁榮）
✓ good	→	**exceptional**（傑出的，優異的）
✓ lucky	→	**fortunate**（幸運的）

由這些例子可以看出，使用初級用字的高層次同義字，便更可以展現該有的意境。

❷ 徹底瞭解單字的「用法」

通常台灣同學在背單字時，僅傾向「瞭解中文意思就夠」。事實上，要徹底瞭解一個單字，包括要瞭解其「用法」才算。比方說，我們在背 expand 一字時，不要想說知道其意是「擴展」就夠了。我們還要學習用這個字來造單詞，比方說 expand my scope of knowledge「擴展知識領域」，或 expand my circle of friends「擴大交友圈」等。如此，今後寫作時，就可以避免僅會寫出 learn new things「學新東西」，或 make new friends「交新朋友」等初級的句子。

只背中文意思：expand ＝ 擴展

進一步學習

徹底了解單字用法：expand my scope of knowledge「擴展知識領域」／
expand my circle of friends「擴大交友圈」

3 多瞭解「片語、慣用語」

　　表達一句英文句子時是很像「中文翻譯」還是「自然英語」，其中便視是否有使用「貼近美語思維」的慣用語而定了。比方說，有同學想表達「塞翁失馬」之意，便直接寫道 Simon lost his horse. 殊不知這樣的句子對讀者是無意義的，美國人是無法瞭解當中意思的。若是以自然的慣用語表示 a blessing in disguise，老外讀者便可輕鬆瞭解意思了。

　　本章節便針對「同義單字」部份來幫同學列出寫作時常使用到的名詞、動詞、形容詞和副詞等各一百組，並列出常使用可以替換的兩個同義字，另也列出常用的「慣用語」一百組。希望協助同學養成「背單字同時想到其同義字」的習慣，以便寫作時有充分的字詞可以運用。

二、動詞 100 組：從「初級字」進階「寫作替換字」

1 動詞第 1-50 組

	初級英語用字	中譯	寫作替換用字 #1	寫作替換用字 #2
1	act	行動	operate	perform
2	add	增加	compute	accumulate
3	agree	同意	comply	recognize
4	allow	許可	approve	authorize
5	ask	詢問	inquire	request
6	begin	開始	commence	establish
7	bet	打賭	venture	speculate
8	bring	帶來	deliver	transport
9	burn	燒	blaze	melt
10	call	叫	signal	command
11	care	照顧	tend	watch

	初級英語用字	中譯	寫作替換用字 #1	寫作替換用字 #2
12	clean	清潔	sweep	cleanse
13	close	關	block	shut
14	collect	收集	compile	gather
15	come	到來	appear	happen
16	copy	複製	imitate	replicate
17	cost	值	require	yield
18	cry	哭	moan	sob
19	cut	切	curtail	slash
20	dare	敢	provoke	resist
21	deal	處理	handle	tackle
22	delay	延遲	hamper	postpone
23	dial	撥打	ring	phone
24	dig	挖	drill	search
25	dive	潛入	leap	plunge
26	do	做	accomplish	achieve
27	draw	拉、拖	elicit	attract
28	dress	穿衣	decorate	attire
29	drink	喝	consume	sip
30	drop	下降	decline	plummet
31	eat	吃	swallow	dine
32	edit	編輯	arrange	compose
33	enjoy	享受	appreciate	adore
34	face	面對	interact	encounter
35	feel	感覺	perceive	sense

	初級英語用字	中譯	寫作替換用字 #1	寫作替換用字 #2
36	file	歸檔	register	classify
37	fill	填入	furnish	supply
38	fix	修理	adjust	restore
39	fly	飛	float	glide
40	forgive	原諒	excuse	absolve
41	get	取得	gain	obtain
42	give	給	donate	provide
43	guess	猜想	suppose	presume
44	hate	討厭	shun	disapprove
45	have	有	acquire	possess
46	help	幫助	stimulate	support
47	hope	希望	anticipate	expect
48	include	包括	encompass	combine
49	invest	投資	devote	endow
50	keep	留住	preserve	retain

EXERCISE 1

請將下列 **10** 個句子改寫為「進階寫作句」！

① That vendor <u>allowed</u> us to sell his products.

✎ _____

② We will <u>bring</u> the package to you tomorrow.

✎ _____

③ Jack <u>came</u> to the door.

✎ _____

④ The weather was bad, so we <u>cut</u> the ceremony early.

✎ _____

⑤ It was snowing very hard, so my bus <u>was delayed</u>.

✎ _____

⑥ If we work hard, we can <u>do</u> many things.

✎ _____

⑦ Interest in our product has <u>dropped</u> over the years.

✎ _____

⑧ Anyone can <u>enjoy</u> their music.

✎ _____

⑨ My father often <u>gives</u> a lot of money to charity.

✎ _____

⑩ We <u>hope</u> the conference will be successful.

✎ _____

EXERCISE 1 · 例解

① The manufacturer <u>authorized</u> us as a dealer to retail his products.
那製造商授權我們經銷他的產品。

② The package will be <u>delivered</u> to you tomorrow.
包裹明天會寄到你手上。

③ Jack suddenly <u>appeared</u> in the doorway.
傑克突然出現在門口。

④ The ceremony had to be <u>curtailed</u> because of the bad weather.
因為氣候不佳之故，慶典要提早結束了。

⑤ Heavy snow <u>hampered</u> the flow of traffic.
大雪阻礙了交通順暢。

⑥ If we all work together, we can <u>accomplish</u> our goal.
若我們同心協力, 就可以達成目標。

⑦ The demand of our product has <u>declined</u> over the years.
過去幾年我們產品的需求下降了。

⑧ Anyone can <u>appreciate</u> their music.
任何人都會喜愛他們的音樂。

⑨ My father frequently <u>donates</u> large sums to charity.
我爸爸經常捐大筆款項給慈善機構。

⑩ We <u>anticipate</u> a successful conference.
我們期待明天的會議成功。

❷ 動詞第 51-100 組

	初級英語用字	中譯	寫作替換用字 #1	寫作替換用字 #2
51	know	知道	realize	comprehend
52	last	持續	continue	extend
53	lead	領導	accompany	conduct
54	learn	學習	master	review
55	like	喜歡	admire	cherish
56	look	看	gaze	stare
57	manage	管理	dominate	regulate
58	mean	意指	represent	imply
59	move	移動	relocate	transfer
60	need	需要	demand	desire
61	notice	察覺	detect	recognize
62	pass	通過	develop	reach
63	pay	付款	compensate	reimburse
64	plan	規劃	organize	blueprint
65	play	玩	perform	present
66	point	指出	indicate	claim
67	print	列印	publish	issue
68	pull	拉	drag	stretch
69	push	推動	accelerate	launch
70	put	放	install	place
71	reach	達到	attain	arrive
72	receive	接收	accept	secure
73	refute	拒絕	oppose	contradict
74	improve	改善	upgrade	recover

	初級英語用字	中譯	寫作替換用字 #1	寫作替換用字 #2
75	request	要求	call for	appeal
76	return	回來	retire	come back
77	run	運作	supervise	operate
78	say	說	announce	reveal
79	see	看	identify	observe
80	shop	買	purchase	hunt for
81	smell	聞	inhale	breathe
82	spend	花費	allocate	contribute
83	start	開始	initiate	create
84	stop	結束	cease	pause
85	suit	適合	correspond	gratify
86	swing	搖擺	fluctuate	curve
87	talk	說	discuss	communicate
88	teach	教	coach	explain
89	throw	丟	pitch	lift
90	travel	旅行	migrate	wander
91	try	試	investigate	evaluate
92	use	使用	employ	exploit
93	vote	投票	elect	choose
94	walk	走路	escort	hike
95	want	想要	aspire	crave
96	waste	浪費	squander	misuse
97	wear	穿戴	display	sport
98	win	贏得	overcome	triumph
99	work	工作	serve	implement
100	yell	喊	roar	shout

請將下列 **10** 個句子改寫為「進階寫作句」！

① I <u>know</u> it's impossible to do this big project.

🖊 _____

② Teachers ask all students to <u>learn</u> English.

🖊 _____

③ Mr. Chen wanted to <u>move</u> the company to China.

🖊 _____

④ He <u>pointed out</u> that he might retire soon.

🖊 _____

⑤ We <u>improved</u> the house by making the kitchen look good.

🖊 _____

⑥ Ms. Smith will <u>say</u> what she is going to do in the meeting.

🖊 _____

⑦ Linda <u>talked</u> to Tom about the details.

🖊 _____

⑧ You should <u>use</u> your skills well.

🖊 _____

⑨ Mr. Wilson <u>wanted</u> to be the president.

✎ _____ •

⑩ We will <u>start working</u> according to new rules.

✎ _____ •

EXERCISE 2 · 例解

① I <u>realize</u> that this ambitious plan can't be achieved.
我發現這個大計劃無法實現。

② Students in Taiwan are expected to <u>master</u> English as a second language.
台灣學生都要學英文當第二外語。

③ Mr. Chen considered <u>relocating</u> the business to China.
陳先生考慮要將公司遷到大陸。

④ He has <u>indicated</u> that he might retire early.
他已指出他可能會提早退休。

⑤ We <u>upgraded</u> the house by updating the kitchen.
我們藉由整修廚房將屋況改善一下。

⑥ Ms. Smith is going to <u>announce</u> her new plan in the meeting.
史密斯女士在會議中要宣佈她的新計劃。

⑦ Linda <u>communicated</u> the details to Tom.
琳達將細節告知湯姆。

⑧ You should fully <u>exploit</u> your talents.
你應該充分運用你的才能。

⑨ Mr. Wilson <u>aspired</u> to the position of president.
威爾森先生期望當總裁。

⑩ We need to <u>implement</u> the new procedures.
我們要執行新的程序。

三、名詞 100 組：從「初級字」進階「寫作替換字」

① 名詞第 1-50 組

	初級英語用字	中譯	寫作替換用字 #1	寫作替換用字 #2
1	activity	活動	exercise	project
2	amount	數量	measure	volume
3	answer	答案	explanation	response
4	argument	爭論	disagreement	controversy
5	attention	注意力	scrutiny	thought
6	average	平均	midpoint	standard
7	background	背景	qualification	credentials
8	balance	平衡	harmony	equity
9	base	基底	infrastructure	foundation
10	beginning	開端	introduction	outset
11	belief	信念	understanding	assumption
12	benefit	好處	advantage	prosperity
13	business	公司、商業	organization	trade
14	cause	起因	motivation	element
15	chance	機會	prospect	opportunity
16	change	改變	transformation	innovation
17	comment	意見	criticism	judgment
18	company	公司	association	community
19	concern	憂慮	involvement	affair
20	confidence	信心	determination	assurance
21	consideration	考慮	deliberation	attention

初級英語用字		中譯	寫作替換用字 #1	寫作替換用字 #2
22	contest	比賽	tournament	challenge
23	coworker	同事	associate	colleague
24	decision	決定	arrangement	resolution
25	difficulty	困難	complication	hardship
26	direction	方向	guidance	administration
27	distance	距離	scope	span
28	education	教育	training	coaching
29	effect	影響	influence	impact
30	emotion	心情	empathy	warmth
31	error	錯誤	flaw	inaccuracy
32	event	活動	occasion	celebration
33	example	例子	illustration	instance
34	exercise	活動	workout	exertion
35	experience	經驗	background	participation
36	expert	專家	professional	authority
37	expression	描述	interpretation	remark
38	feeling	感覺	awareness	sensitivity
39	form	形式	pattern	scheme
40	fortune	好運	affluence	prosperity
41	friend	朋友	acquaintance	companion
42	goal	目標	target	objective
43	grade	成績	rank	quality
44	growth	成長	advance	improvement
45	health	健康	strength	well-being

	初級英語用字	中譯	寫作替換用字 #1	寫作替換用字 #2
46	homework	作業	assignment	practice
47	idea	意見	feedback	opinion
48	improvement	改進	enhancement	progress
49	income	收入	compensation	payoff
50	interest	興趣	enthusiasm	pursuit

EXERCISE 3

請將下列 **10** 個句子改寫為「進階寫作句」！

① No one gave <u>answers</u> to Mr. Chen's remarks.

    🖉 _____

② Mr. Chen's <u>qualifications and background</u> is suitable for the job.

    🖉 _____

③ Speaking English is a great <u>benefit</u>.

    🖉 _____

④ Mr. Chen asks us for new ideas for making <u>changes</u>.

    🖉 _____

⑤ Linda is joining the tennis <u>contest</u>.

    🖉 _____

⑥ Parents tell their children what <u>direction</u> to go in.

    🖉 _____

⑦ This report had many <u>errors</u>.

    🖉 _____

⑧ Jack is an <u>expert</u> in golf.

    🖉 _____

⑨ My <u>goal</u> is to become a leader.

✐ _____

⑩ We don't know what our customers' <u>ideas</u> are.

✐ _____

EXERCISE 3 · 例解

① There has been no <u>response</u> to Mr. Chen's remarks.
沒有人對陳先生的評論做出反應。

② Mr. Chen has the right <u>credentials</u> for the position.
陳先生有資格做這個職位。

③ It will be to your <u>advantage</u> to master English.
精通英文會是你的優勢。

④ Mr. Chen promotes originality and encourages <u>innovation</u>.
陳先生宣導原創性並鼓勵創新。

⑤ Linda will be playing in the next tennis <u>tournament</u>.
琳達會在下一場網路賽中出賽。

⑥ Most young people depend on their parents for <u>guidance</u>.
多數年輕人都依賴父母的引導。

⑦ This report contained many <u>inaccuracies</u>.
此報告包括許多錯誤。

⑧ Jack is truly a golf <u>professional</u>.
傑克真的是高爾夫球專家。

⑨ To be a leader is one of my long-term <u>objectives</u>.
當老闆是我長期目標之一。

⑩ We don't get much <u>feedback</u> from customers.
我們得自客戶的回饋意見並不多。

❷ 名詞第 51-100 組

	初級英語用字	中譯	寫作替換用字 #1	寫作替換用字 #2
51	item	物品、成份	component	piece
52	job	工作	occupation	career
53	leader	領導人	chief	conductor
54	lesson	課程	instruction	lecture
55	meeting	會議	convention	conference
56	method	方式	approach	technique
57	mistake	錯誤	oversight	fault
58	moment	時刻	stage	point in time
59	money	錢	capital	property
60	partner	夥伴	teammate	associate
61	pattern	模式	sequence	system
62	person	個人	individual	character
63	pleasure	愉悅	contentment	satisfaction
64	policy	政策	guideline	regulation
65	preference	偏好	alternative	inclination
66	problem	問題	obstacle	dilemma
67	profile	輪廓	portrait	sketch
68	program	計劃	curriculum	project
69	progress	進展	breakthrough	evolution
70	promise	承諾	pledge	affirmation
71	proof	證據	evidence	verification
72	public	大眾	population	audience
73	question	問題	inquiry	confusion
74	reason	原因	logic	rationale

	初級英語用字	中譯	寫作替換用字 #1	寫作替換用字 #2
75	reference	參考資料	quotation	endorsement
76	relief	解除	relaxation	remedy
77	research	研究	exploration	analysis
78	response	回應	feedback	acknowledgment
79	result	結果	outcome	conclusion
80	rule	規定	principle	command
81	schedule	時刻表	itinerary	timetable
82	sector	區塊	region	district
83	service	服務	assistance	courtesy
84	specialist	專員	technician	consultant
85	speech	演講	address	presentation
86	standard	標準	specification	norm
87	statement	聲明	declaration	announcement
88	strength	力量	vitality	durability
89	subject	科目	theme	business matter
90	surprise	驚訝	marvel	amazement
91	survey	調查	inspection	analysis
92	system	系統	structure	logical order
93	team	團隊	group	unit
94	thing	東西、某事	concept	material
95	topic	主題	proposition	thesis
96	trade	貿易	commerce	exchange
97	tradition	傳統	culture	ritual
98	training	訓練	education	drill
99	value	價值	significance	meaning
100	way	方法	scheme	strategy

EXERCISE 4

請將下列 **10** 個句子改寫為「進階寫作句」！

① I want a <u>job</u> which lets me use English.

✐ _____

② The <u>meeting</u> for all managers will be in Tokyo.

✐ _____

③ Our company lacks <u>money</u>.

✐ _____

④ One <u>person</u> can't do such a big thing.

✐ _____

⑤ There is no <u>proof</u> the theory is right.

✐ _____

⑥ The <u>result</u> of our discussion is to sell products to other countries.

✐ _____

⑦ We can run this charity because many people provide <u>service</u>.

✐ _____

⑧ This film's <u>subject</u> is talking about young and old people's conflict.

✐ _____

⑨ I added many <u>things</u> to the story.

🖉 _____ •

⑩ We have new <u>ways</u> to do marketing.

🖉 _____ •

EXERCISE 4 · 例解

① I'm looking for an <u>occupation</u> which will allow me to apply my English ability.
我希望找的工作是可以讓我應用英文實力。

② The management <u>conference</u> will be held in Tokyo.
管理會議將在東京舉辦。

③ Our company is having difficulties in raising <u>capital</u>.
我們公司在籌錢方面遇到困難。

④ A single <u>individual</u> is not likely to achieve all this.
單獨一個人不太可能完成所有事。

⑤ There is no <u>evidence</u> to support this theory.
沒有證據來支持此理論。

⑥ The <u>outcome</u> of our discussion is to expand international markets.
我們討論的結果是要拓展國際市場。

⑦ We've been operating the charity with the <u>assistance</u> of volunteers.
我們營運這慈善機構有很多志工的協助。

⑧ The central <u>theme</u> of this film is the conflict between young and old people.
此電影的中心主題是年輕人與老一代的衝突。

⑨ I have added some new <u>material</u> to the story.
我為此故事增加了些新素材。

⑩ We've come up with new marketing <u>strategies</u>.
我們已想出新的行銷策略了。

1 形容詞第 1-50 組

	初級英語用字	中譯	寫作替換用字 #1	寫作替換用字 #2
1	active	活動的	effective	alive
2	angry	生氣的	furious	annoyed
3	bad	不好的	negative	unacceptable
4	beautiful	美麗的	gorgeous	appealing
5	big	大的	enormous	substantial
6	brave	勇敢的	fearless	adventurous
7	brief	簡明的	concise	sharp
8	busy	忙碌的	unavailable	engaged
9	calm	沉穩的	tranquil	soothing
10	careful	小心的	attentive	mindful
11	cheap	便宜的	economical	reasonable
12	clean	乾淨的	hygienic	orderly
13	cold	冷的	frigid	frozen
14	colorful	多彩的	vivid	flashy
15	common	一般的	prevalent	typical
16	crazy	瘋狂的	insane	lunatic
17	dark	黑暗的	gloomy	overcast
18	deep	深沉的	profound	broad
19	delicious	美味的	tempting	appetizing
20	detailed	細節的	precise	thorough
21	different	不同的	distinctive	particular

	初級英語用字	中譯	寫作替換用字 #1	寫作替換用字 #2
22	dirty	骯髒的	messy	sloppy
23	dry	乾燥的	dehydrated	arid
24	dull	無趣的	boring	sluggish
25	early	早的	previous	initial
26	easy	簡單的	straightforward	obvious
27	empty	空的	vacant	blank
28	exciting	興奮的	intriguing	impressive
29	expensive	昂貴的	costly	overpriced
30	famous	有名的	glorious	outstanding
31	fast	快速的	rapid	swift
32	fat	胖的	obese	plump
33	few	少的	slight	minor
34	flat	平的	plane	horizontal
35	fresh	新鮮的	natural	recent
36	friendly	友善的	amiable	affable
37	enough	足夠的	complete	sufficient
38	funny	有趣的	entertaining	amusing
39	gentle	溫和的	moderate	tame
40	good	好的	exceptional	marvelous
41	great	棒的	extreme	considerable
42	handsome	帥氣的	elegant	stylish
43	happy	高興的	cheerful	delighted
44	hard	硬的	solid	tough
45	harmful	有害的	destructive	damaging

	初級英語用字	中譯	寫作替換用字 #1	寫作替換用字 #2
46	healthy	健康的	hearty	robust
47	heavy	重的	bulky	excessive
48	helpful	有幫助的	invaluable	supportive
49	high	高的	immense	tremendous
50	honest	誠實的	sincere	reliable

EXERCISE 5

請將下列 **10** 個句子改寫為「進階寫作句」！

① Linda gave me a <u>bad</u> answer.

    🖉 _____•

② Mr. Chen has a <u>big</u> house.

    🖉 _____•

③ I'm very <u>busy</u> doing two projects.

    🖉 _____•

④ This book has <u>deep</u> meaning.

    🖉 _____•

⑤ I feel <u>dull</u> in the evening.

    🖉 _____•

⑥ We need to decide <u>fast</u>.

    🖉 _____•

⑦ He has <u>enough</u> money and can retire soon.

    🖉 _____•

⑧ She is <u>good</u> at playing the piano.

    🖉 _____•

⑨ We see you again and feel very <u>happy</u>.

✎ _____ •

⑩ Mr. Chen gives us a lot of very <u>helpful</u> information.

✎ _____ •

EXERCISE 5 · 例解

① Linda gave a vague but <u>negative</u> response.
琳達給了不明確的否定答案。

② Mr. Chen lives in an <u>enormous</u> mansion.
陳先生住在寬敞的宅邸中。

③ I'm currently <u>engaged</u> in two projects.
我目前忙於兩個案子中。

④ This book is full of <u>profound</u> insights.
這本書內有很多影響深遠的見地。

⑤ I always feel a bit <u>sluggish</u> in the evenings.
一到晚上我總覺得有點消沉。

⑥ We need to make a <u>swift</u> decision.
我們要很快做個決定。

⑦ He has <u>sufficient</u> income to retire comfortably.
他有足夠收入可以過舒服的退休生活了。

⑧ Her piano playing is <u>exceptional</u>.
她的鋼琴演奏非常優異。

⑨ We are <u>delighted</u> to meet you again.
我們很高興再次見到你。

⑩ Mr. Chen is an <u>invaluable</u> source of information.
陳先生總會提供無價的寶貴經驗。

❷ 形容詞第 51-100 組

	初級英語用字	中譯	寫作替換用字 #1	寫作替換用字 #2
51	important	重要的	essential	vital
52	interesting	有趣的	alluring	attractive
53	jealous	妒忌的	envious	envying
54	kind	和善的	sympathetic	compassionate
55	large	大的	generous	massive
56	late	遲的	delayed	lagging
57	lazy	懶惰的	passive	idle
58	light	光亮的	bright	shiny
59	lucky	幸運的	fortunate	blessed
60	main	主要的	leading	primary
61	many	很多的	countless	various
62	modern	現代的	state-of-the-art	contemporary
63	next to	鄰近的	adjacent	neighboring
64	nervous	緊張的	concerned	irritable
65	new	新的	advanced	latest
66	nice	好的	pleasant	charming
67	noisy	吵鬧的	disorderly	rowdy
68	old	舊的	ancient	mature
69	poor	可憐的	needy	miserable
70	powerful	有權力的	influential	compelling
71	pretty	美的	graceful	delicate
72	proud	驕傲的	appreciative	noble
73	pure	純粹的	transparent	simple
74	quick	快的	energetic	sudden

	初級英語用字	中譯	寫作替換用字 #1	寫作替換用字 #2
75	quiet	安靜的	peaceful	silent
76	real	真正的	authentic	absolute
77	rich	有錢的	wealthy	affluent
78	right	正確的	appropriate	suitable
79	sad	難過的	pessimistic	heartbroken
80	safe	安全的	protected	secure
81	same	相同的	equivalent	look-alike
82	shy	害羞的	hesitant	timid
83	small	小的	limited	miniature
84	smart	聰明的	brilliant	genius
85	soft	柔和的	mild	flexible
86	strong	強壯的	vigorous	durable
87	stupid	愚昧的	foolish	senseless
88	super	傑出的	outstanding	topnotch
89	sweet	甜的	sugared	delicious
90	tiny	小的	insignificant	negligible
91	tired	累的	exhausted	fatigued
92	ugly	醜的	awful	unattractive
93	useful	有用的	practical	conducive
94	warm	溫暖的	sweating	heated
95	weak	弱的	fragile	unsteady
96	wet	濕的	humid	soaked
97	wide	廣的	far-reaching	spacious
98	worried	擔心的	disturbed	distressed
99	wrong	錯誤的	inaccurate	mistaken
100	young	年輕的	inexperienced	junior

EXERCISE 6

請將下列 **10** 個句子改寫為「進階寫作句」！

① Love is <u>important</u> to children.

✎ _____

② That building is very <u>large</u>.

✎ _____

③ I feel I am very <u>lucky</u>.

✎ _____

④ The fire quickly burned other buildings <u>next to</u> it.

✎ _____

⑤ They live in very <u>poor</u> conditions.

✎ _____

⑥ We need a <u>quiet</u> way to solve this problem.

✎ _____

⑦ Mr. Chen is getting <u>rich</u>.

✎ _____

⑧ That method is very <u>smart</u>.

✎ _____

⑨ Mary Jones is a <u>super</u> star.

✎ _____ •

⑩ He is thinking about a <u>useful</u> solution.

✎ _____ •

EXERCISE 6 · 例解

① Love is an <u>essential</u> part of children's development.
愛對小孩成長來說是重要的一環。

② It certainly is a <u>massive</u> building.
那真的是一棟很壯觀的建築。

③ I have had a very <u>fortunate</u> life.
我這輩子都還滿幸運的。

④ The fire quickly spread to <u>adjacent</u> buildings.
大火很快地延燒到鄰近的建築了。

⑤ They are living in <u>miserable</u> conditions.
他們過著悲慘的生活。

⑥ We are seeking a <u>peaceful</u> solution to this conflict.
我們要找和平解決問題的方式。

⑦ Mr. Chen is becoming even more <u>affluent</u> than before.
陳先生變得比之前更富有了。

⑧ That's a <u>brilliant</u> solution to the problem.
那真是個聰明的解決問題的辦法。

⑨ Mary Jones is an <u>outstanding</u> actress.
瑪莉瓊斯是個傑出的女演員。

⑩ He's trying to find a <u>practical</u> solution to the problem.
他試著要找出問題的合理答案。

五、副詞 100 組：從「初級字」進階「寫作替換字」

❶ 副詞第 1-50 組

	初級英語用字	中譯	寫作替換用字 #1	寫作替換用字 #2
1	about	約略	approximately	around
2	actually	事實上地	indeed	literally
3	badly	不佳地	unfortunately	awkwardly
4	beautifully	美麗地	gorgeously	appealingly
5	busily	忙碌地、辛勤地	diligently	energetically
6	carefully	謹慎地	attentively	thoughtfully
7	cleanly	乾淨地	neatly	spotlessly
8	clearly	清楚地	apparently	obviously
9	closely	接近地	intimately	strictly
10	coldly	冷漠地	heartlessly	indifferently
11	colorfully	鮮艷多彩地	merrily	splendidly
12	commonly	普通地	generally	regularly
13	crazily	瘋狂地	madly	wildly
14	deeply	深沉地	profoundly	severely
15	differently	不同地、多變地	separately	variously
16	directly	直接地	immediately	promptly
17	early	提早	timely	right away
18	easily	輕易地	effortlessly	handily
19	equally	公平地	fairly	impartially
20	especially	特殊地	specifically	remarkably
21	evenly	公平地	precisely	justly

	初級英語用字	中譯	寫作替換用字 #1	寫作替換用字 #2
22	exactly	確切地	definitely	absolutely
23	fairly	公正地	reasonably	averagely
24	fast	快速地	rapidly	swiftly
25	finally	最終	completely	eventually
26	forever	永久	constantly	endlessly
27	formally	正式地	officially	properly
28	frankly	坦白地	bluntly	honestly
29	freely	開放地、自由地	openly	liberally
30	fully	全然地	entirely	perfectly
31	generally	一般地	normally	practically
32	gently	溫和地	mildly	tenderly
33	gladly	欣喜地	gratefully	delightedly
34	greatly	很棒地	incredibly	markedly
35	handily	輕易地	skillfully	cleverly
36	happily	快樂地	agreeably	lovingly
37	healthily	健康地	actively	hardily
38	highly	高度地、非常	extremely	immensely
39	honestly	真誠地	truly	naturally
40	hopefully	期望地	expectantly	optimistically
41	hugely	引人注目地	excessively	strikingly
42	incorrectly	不正確地	wrongly	falsely
43	just	僅僅、只是	simply	merely
44	kindly	心善地	politely	graciously
45	eventually	最終地	finally	ultimately

	初級英語用字	中譯	寫作替換用字 #1	寫作替換用字 #2
46	late	晚、遲到	tardily	slowly
47	lately	最近地	newly	recently
48	less	僅只	barely	meagerly
49	lightly	輕微地	slightly	casually
50	likely	可能地	probably	presumably

EXERCISE 7

請將下列 10 個句子改寫為「進階寫作句」！

① We spent <u>about</u> two hours in the meeting.

🖉 _____ •

② Everyone listened <u>carefully</u>.

🖉 _____ •

③ I know my friends <u>closely</u>.

🖉 _____ •

④ The kid went to sleep <u>directly</u>.

🖉 _____ •

⑤ I want to know why Linda can <u>easily</u> learn a language.

🖉 _____ •

⑥ The price of those clothes are <u>fairly</u> good.

🖉 _____ •

⑦ These two cases are not <u>fully</u> the same.

🖉 _____ •

⑧ Smart-phones are <u>highly</u> common today.

🖉 _____ •

⑨ <u>Eventually</u> we will need to buy our own house.

✎ _____ •

⑩ Linda has <u>likely</u> left the office already.

✎ _____ •

📦 EXERCISE 7 · 例解

① The meeting lasted <u>approximately</u> two hours.
會議開了大約兩小時。

② The team members all listened <u>attentively</u>.
所有同仁都很仔細地聽。

③ I get to know my friends <u>intimately</u>.
我對朋友瞭解至深。

④ The kid lay down and <u>promptly</u> fell asleep.
那小孩躺下，很快地就睡著了。

⑤ I wonder why Linda can learn a foreign language <u>effortlessly</u>.
我想知道琳達如何可以不費力地學會外語。

⑥ Those clothes are <u>reasonably</u> priced.
這些衣服定價都很合理。

⑦ These two projects are <u>entirely</u> different.
那兩個案子全然不同。

⑧ Smart-phones are <u>extremely</u> prevalent nowadays.
現今智慧手機已極度地普遍使用了。

⑨ We <u>ultimately</u> need to buy a house of our own.
我們最終還是要買自己的房子。

⑩ Linda is not in the office – <u>presumably</u> she left already.
琳達不在辦公室，可能提早離開了吧。

② 副詞第 51-100 組

	初級英語用字	中譯	寫作替換用字 #1	寫作替換用字 #2
51	loosely	約略地	roughly	relatively
52	loudly	大聲地、吵雜地	noisily	powerfully
53	luckily	幸運地	fortunately	favorably
54	mainly	主要地	primarily	essentially
55	merely	僅僅、只是	hardly	simply
56	mostly	主要地	frequently	principally
57	nearly	幾乎	virtually	in the ballpark
58	never	從未	not at all	at no time
59	next	接著	afterward	behind
60	nicely	良好地	attractively	charmingly
61	normally	正常地	typically	ordinarily
62	often	時常	oftentimes	regularly
63	once	一度	previously	before
64	only	僅有	solely	alone
65	openly	開放地、自由地	fact to face	readily
66	partially	部份地	somewhat	moderately
67	perfectly	全然地	altogether	utterly
68	personally	私人地	privately	subjectively
69	poorly	不足地	insufficiently	inadequately
70	possibly	可能地	by any means	perhaps
71	probably	可能地	doubtless	plausibly
72	quickly	迅速地	hurriedly	instantly
73	quietly	安靜地	silently	secretly
74	quite	非常	totally	in reality

	初級英語用字	中譯	寫作替換用字 #1	寫作替換用字 #2
75	rarely	稀少地	seldom	notably
76	readily	輕易地	no sweat	in no time
77	really	眞正地	undoubtedly	legitimately
78	recently	最近地	freshly	just a while ago
79	rudely	粗暴地	harshly	crudely
80	sadly	難過地	gloomily	sorrowfully
81	safely	安全地	harmlessly	guardedly
82	seldom	鮮少	occasionally	once in a while
83	sharply	激烈地	strongly	distinctly
84	shortly	簡短地	proximately	briefly
85	simply	簡易地	straightforwardly	in fact
86	slightly	輕微地	to some extent	marginally
87	softly	溫和地	smoothly	gradually
88	solely	單獨地	exclusively	single-handedly
89	sometimes	有時	from time to time	periodically
90	especially	特別地、尤其	uniquely	particularly
91	successfully	成功地	thrivingly	flourishingly
92	surely	確定地	evidently	inevitably
93	totally	全然地	unconditionally	comprehensively
94	truly	眞正地	without a doubt	firmly
95	very	非常	noticeably	pretty
96	well	很棒地	effectively	proficiently
97	wholly	全然地	in every respect	outright
98	widely	廣大地	extensively	universally
99	willingly	自願地	voluntarily	gladly
100	wonderfully	很棒地	stunningly	admirably

EXERCISE 8

請將下列 10 個句子改寫為「進階寫作句」！

① Their money is <u>mainly</u> from farming.

   ✎ _____

② That garden is designed <u>nicely</u>.

   ✎ _____

③ Ms. Jones and Linda will meet <u>personally</u> next Monday.

   ✎ _____

④ I'm <u>rarely</u> treated with rudeness.

   ✎ _____

⑤ Everyone agrees that Mr. Jones is a <u>really</u> good speaker.

   ✎ _____

⑥ Jones finished that project <u>solely</u>. It's unbelievable.

   ✎ _____

⑦ I <u>especially</u> like novels.

   ✎ _____

⑧ Mr. Chen is <u>surely</u> angry.

   ✎ _____

⑨ This book is <u>totally</u> full of pictures.

🖉 _____•

⑩ Mr. Jones has answered the question <u>well</u>.

🖉 _____•

EXERCISE 8 · 例解

① Their income is <u>primarily</u> from farming.
他們的收入主要來自農作。

② That is really an <u>attractively</u> designed garden.
這真的是一個設計迷人的花園。

③ Ms. Jones will meet Linda <u>privately</u> next Monday.
瓊斯小姐下週一會與琳達私下會面。

④ I've <u>seldom</u> experienced such rudeness.
我鮮少受到如此粗魯的對待。

⑤ Mr. Jones is <u>undoubtedly</u> a great speaker.
瓊斯先生無疑是最棒的演說者。

⑥ I can't believe Jones has completed that project <u>single-handedly</u>.
真不敢相信瓊斯獨力將那專案完成了。

⑦ I <u>particularly</u> enjoy reading novels.
我尤其喜歡讀小說。

⑧ Mr. Chen is quite <u>evidently</u> furious.
陳先生很顯然是生了大氣。

⑨ This story book is <u>comprehensively</u> illustrated.
此故事書整本都有附插圖。

⑩ Mr. Jones has <u>effectively</u> addressed the topic.
瓊斯先生有效地針對主題回答了。

❶ 片語第 1-50 組

	常用慣用語	中文涵意
1	a back-handed compliment	言不由衷的讚美，虛假的讚美
2	a long face	拉長著臉，垮著臉
3	a bed of roses	安樂窩，順遂的境遇
4	a blessing in disguise	塞翁失馬，焉知非福
5	a bolt from the blue	晴天霹靂
6	a bosom pal	知音朋友
7	a breath of fresh air	耳目一新，感覺新鮮
8	a bull in a china shop	魯莽闖禍之人
9	a cock-and-bull story	荒謬故事，無稽之談
10	a dead end	窮途末路
11	a fair-weather friend	酒肉朋友
12	a fat chance	機會渺茫
13	a finger in every pie	凡事都要插手
14	a golden opportunity	絕佳的機會
15	a grey area	灰色地帶
16	a straight face	表情嚴肅，正經八百
17	a wet blanket	掃興
18	absent-minded	精神恍惚，注意力不集中
19	alive and kicking	活蹦亂跳
20	all ears	仔細聆聽，全神貫注
21	all eyes	聚精會神

	常用慣用語	中文涵意
22	at the eleventh hour	及時，最後一刻
23	back-breaking	精疲力竭，累攤了
24	bad blood	仇視，敵對
25	bark up the wrong tree	問錯人了
26	bear in mind	記得，時常提醒
27	beat about the bush	兜圈子，沒講重點
28	behind closed doors	關起門來，私底下，與世隔絕
29	behind my back	背地裡，台面下
30	bite off more than you can chew	不自量力，貪多嚼不爛
31	blow your own trumpet	自吹自擂
32	break the ice	破冰，打破沉默
33	break your word	食言，未守承諾
34	breathe down my neck	在我身後東窺西探
35	burn a hole in my pocket	有錢就花完，留不住錢財
36	burn the candle at both ends	蠟燭兩頭燒
37	burn the midnight oil	熬夜，開夜車
38	by word of mouth	口耳相傳
39	carry the can	負擔責任，替人受過
40	castles in the air	白日夢，不可能實現之事
41	catch my attention	引起我的注意
42	catch someone red-handed	逮個正著
43	child's play	兒戲，輕而易舉之事
44	comfort zone	舒適圈
45	cool my heels	等很久，讓人久等

	常用慣用語	中文涵意
46	crocodile tears	假慈悲
47	daylight robbery	貴得離譜
48	drop the subject	停止討論，換個話題
49	eat my words	承認之前說錯話
50	face the music	面對事實

EXERCISE 9

請為下列 **10** 個片語造句！

① long face

✎ _____

② a blessing in disguise

✎ _____

③ a fair-weather friend

✎ _____

④ a golden opportunity

✎ _____

⑤ alive and kicking

✎ _____

⑥ bark up the wrong tree

✎ _____

⑦ break the ice

✎ _____

⑧ by word of mouth

✎ _____

⑨ child's play

   ✎ _____

⑩ daylight robbery

   ✎ _____

EXERCISE 9 · 例解

① Why have you got such a long face? Cheer up!
為何拉長著臉呢？振作一點！

② Losing my job turned out to be a blessing in disguise.
丟了工作到後來變成是塞翁失馬焉知非福了。

③ A fair-weather friend isn't much help in an emergency.
酒肉朋友在緊急狀況下是不會提供多少幫助的。

④ Jack has missed his golden opportunity to win that case.
傑克已失去可贏得案子的絕佳機會。

⑤ Linda has completely recovered, and she is alive and kicking now.
琳達已完全康復了，她現在生龍活虎的。

⑥ If you think I can lend you more money, you're barking up the wrong tree.
若你認為我會再多借點錢給你，那你可就錯了。

⑦ A nice warm smile does a lot to break the ice.
一個美好溫暖的微笑對消除冰冷氣氛有很大作用。

⑧ We don't do marketing, but the buzz about our products get spread by word of mouth.
我們沒做行銷，但關於我們產品的訊息都是口耳相傳的。

⑨ Finding the right street is child's play with Google Map.
有了 Google Map 工具，要找正確的街道可是很簡單的。

⑩ The cost of renting a car at the airport is daylight robbery.
在機場租車簡直是貴得離譜呀！

1 片語第 51-100 組

	常用慣用語	中文涵意
51	fight a losing battle	從事無勝算的鬥爭
52	foot a bill	付款，付帳
53	from scratch	從頭開始
54	from the bottom of my heart	打從心底
55	get back on my own feet	靠自己重新振作
56	get cold feet	臨陣退縮
57	get out of bed on the wrong side	整天脾氣不好
58	get the ball rolling	動起來，蓬勃發展起來
59	give m the cold shoulder	刻意冷淡，無視我的存在
60	give someone a big hand	提供某人協助
61	give the game away	揭露秘密
62	go up in the world	飛黃騰達
63	have a bee in your bonnet	念念不忘，一直想，揮之不去
64	have a chip on my shoulder	個性好鬥，脾氣很衝
65	have an ace up your sleeve	秘密武器，致勝關鍵
66	have an axe to grind	別有用心，另有企圖
67	hit the nail on the head	一針見血
68	hot air	廢話
69	in black and white	白紙黑字寫下
70	in cold blood	冷血，蓄意
71	in my bad books	在我不喜歡的人之列（非我喜歡之人）
72	in the black	有賺錢，盈餘
73	in the dark	背地裡，黑暗中
74	in the red	赤字，負債

	常用慣用語	中文涵意
75	in the twinkling of an eye	一轉眼的功夫
76	keep your chin up	振作，樂觀以對
77	kill two birds with one stone	一石二鳥
78	lay down your arms	停火，投降
79	live from hand to mouth	過著勉強糊口的生活
80	make the grade	成功
81	mind your own business	管好自己的事，勿插手他人之事
82	not my cup of tea	不是我的菜
83	not the end of the world	不是世界末日，沒什麼大不了
84	on the breadline	勉強糊口，過著窮困的生活
85	pass the buck	踢皮球
86	pay it by ear	且看且走
87	rain cats and dogs	下傾盆大雨
88	round the clock	日以繼夜，不斷地
89	the apple of my eye	摯愛，掌上明珠
90	the black market	黑市
91	the generation gap	代溝
92	the man in the street	一般人，老百姓
93	till the cows come home	長時間等待，直到天荒地老，無期限
94	under the weather	身體欠安
95	up in arms	激列反對
96	ups and downs	起伏
97	walk on air	心情愉悅，高興
98	wear many hats	身兼數職
99	with flying colors	大獲全勝
100	with your bare hands	赤手空拳

EXERCISE 10

請為下列 10 個片語造句！

① from scratch

✐_____

② get the ball rolling

✐_____

③ go up in the world

✐_____

④ in black and white

✐_____

⑤ in the black

✐_____

⑥ keep your chin up

✐_____

⑦ make the grade

✐_____

⑧ pass the buck

✐_____

⑨ under the weather

✎ _____ •

⑩ with flying colors

✎ _____ •

Exercise 10 · 例解

① They lost everything in the fire and had to start again from scratch.
他們在火災中失去一切，只好從頭開始。

② Let's get the ball rolling by putting up some posters.
讓我們動起來，先將海報貼一貼吧。

③ Jones really went up in the world after he won the lottery.
瓊斯贏得樂透之後真的就發展起來了。

④ The agreement is good, but the manager wants it put in black and white.
有共識是很好，但老闆想要將要點白紙黑字寫下來。

⑤ Mr. Jones successfully moved the company in the black.
瓊斯先生成功地帶領公司轉虧為盈。

⑥ Keep your chin up and everything will get better.
樂觀點，所有事都會變好的。

⑦ This report doesn't just make the grade. It's excellent.
這份報告不僅寫得好而已，是真的很棒。

⑧ Parents tend to pass the buck to teachers when their children misbehave in school.
小孩在校行為偏差時，父母傾向將責任推給老師。

⑨ It's hard to perform well when you're under the weather.
若身體不適就難以表現良好。

⑩ Joe passed his English exam with flying colors.
裘高分通過英文測驗。

UNIT 2 → 文法句型

　　筆者數年來修改過的英文寫作不下數千篇，發覺多數同學在文法句型方面的問題也呈 M 型化發展出兩大類：

A. 基本文法概念薄弱

　　一句子內的主詞動詞單複數不一致，出現數個動詞，甚至一長句跨了三四行，僅是文字隨意組合起來，隨便以逗號隔開而已。如此無文法無句型的句子，會導致讀者完全無法會意，考試時還會被視為嚴重的錯誤而扣分。

　　針對這類「文法弱底」的同學，建議要寫作之前先「求對」，將國中與高中的「基本文法概念」加強好，包括：主詞的選擇，動詞的變化，形容詞／副詞的作用，關係子句，倒裝句……等概念都先弄得一清二楚。若基本句子都沒法成型，光用文字拼湊出言不及意的句子，是沒有意義的。（此書專門討論寫作本身，與講述「文法規則」有些區隔，為了避免同學又陷入「被文法規則搞昏」的情況，本書內沒有收錄細部文法解說。）

B. 使用中文思維來套用英文句型

　　另一類同學基本文法概念都有了，寫句子時細節文法規則已鮮少出現錯誤，但問題出現在：句子內文法都對，但看起來就還是有「中式英文」的感覺。

　　針對這類已有基本文法基礎的同學要「求好」，先將自己想要表達的句子寫下（可能有中式感覺無妨），然後再細節調整：我這句子的主詞精準嗎？是在講何時的事？動詞變化正確嗎？用字有符合我原始的語意嗎？還是用了無法搭配前後文、不恰當的字了呢？

　　除了要有「自我修改」之能力外，針對這類「求對之後，還要求好求精」的同學，可以練習套用以下的「英文句型」來表達意思。若沒有英文句型可套用，那受到

中文母語干擾的同學，自然會一直朝向中文句型來寫英文句子了。但若有如以下的英文句型可以套用的話，同學僅需把配合自己意思的用字代入句型中即可，便顯得簡單得多了。

　　舉個簡單的例子：針對「我不想做那工作。」這句，我們一般都想直接翻成 I don't want to do the job. 但若有句型 S. + be reluctant to + [do something]. 可套用的話，就可以套入形成這樣的句子：I am reluctant to do the job. 接著可以再將文字 do the job 美化一下，形成：I am reluctant to take on the responsibility. 這個沒有中文味的句子了。由此可知，有現成英文句型給我們套用之後，寫句子是不是就變得簡單又不失英文原味了呢？

　　本章節第二部分所列的是最常用的 80 組句型，從表達意見、舉例、到結論可使用的句型都有包含。每句都有三個範例句，最重要的是，同學瞭解句型後要親自練習，套用句型寫下符合自身意見的句子喔！

一、寫作常用訊號字分類

❶ To give an opinion（陳述意見）

General（一般用字）	Advanced alternatives（進階選擇）
I believe…（我相信……）	**I'd like to explain why…** （讓我解釋……的原因……）
I consider…（我認為……）	**I am convinced that…**（我相信……）
I personally think that…（我個人認為……）	**I hold that…**（我堅信……）
I'd prefer…（我偏好……）	**I deem…**（我視……為……）
In my opinion…（在我看來……）	**I assert…**（我堅持……）
It seems to me that…（在我來看……）	**As far as I'm concerned…** （就……而言……）
I suggest…（我建議……）	
To start with,…（首先……）	**Undeniably…**（不可否認的……）
About this matter…（關於此議題……）	**It is obvious that…**（很明顯的……）

Concerning…（關於……）	**To tell the truth,**（講實在的……）
With regard to…（關於……）	**To be frank,**（坦白說……）
People say that…（人們認為……）	**Frankly speaking,**（坦白說……）
They say that…（大家會說……）	
It is said that…（一般相信……）	

❷ To state the reason（解釋原因）

General（一般用字）	Advanced alternatives（進階選擇）
There are various reasons why… （關於……有數個原因……）	**We must draw attention to…** （我們要注意……）
There are several explanations for… （關於……有數個解釋……）	**We should not overlook…** （我們不能忽略……）
There are many positive reasons for… （關於……有很多正面的理由……）	**The important point to note is…** （要注意的要點是……）
There are more benefits to… （對……有更多好處……）	**I offer here some reasons why…** （我提供幾個原因……）
There are a number of reasons for… （針對……有幾個原因……）	**The reason for this is not hard to see: it is…** （對此……原因就不難看出了……）

❸ To set up a condition（設立條件）

General（一般用字）	Advanced alternatives（進階選擇）
If…（假若……） Even if…（即便……） If I could…（若我可以……）	**Whether or not…**（不論……） **This might cause…**（這可能會……）

❹ To add extra information（提供更多資訊）

General（一般用字）	Advanced alternatives（進階選擇）
First of all… Second… Next… Lastly…（首先…… 第二……接著……最後……）	Still less, …（還有……）
In addition…（除此之外……）	And that is not all.（還不僅如此……）
And… then…（接著……）	More examples can be found in…（還有更多例子……）
There are three reasons why…（對此原因有三……）	Not only… but also…（不僅……還……）
Similarly…（相同地……）	Additionally…（除此之外……）
Furthermore…（甚至於……）	Alternatively…（再者……）
Moreover…（更甚者……）	… as well as…（也……和……）
Further…（另外……）	… equally important…（同等重要……）
What's more…（更甚者……）	… not to mention…（更別說……）
More than…（比……更……）	On top of this…（更重要的是……）
Also…（而且……）	
Both… and…（兩者…… 都……）	
Besides that,（此外……）	

❺ To generalize（述說一般事件）

General（一般用字）	Advanced alternatives（進階選擇）
Overall…（總的來說……）	Theoretically…（理論上……）
In general…（一般說來……）	Hypothetically…（假設說……）
Generally speaking…（一般來看……）	Traditionally…（傳統上……）
For the most part…（很多時候……）	Broadly speaking…（大抵上……）
Usually…（通常……）	Strictly speaking…（嚴格來說……）
Normally…（一般狀況下……）	It goes without saying that…（不可否認地……）
	Needless to say …（不需多說……）
	It is quite obvious that…（很顯然地……）

❻ To restate an Argument（重述論點）

General（一般用字）	Advanced alternatives（進階選擇）
To repeat…（再一次……） In other words…（也就是說……） That means…（這就意味……） To put it in another way…（換言之……）	**To put it differently…** （換個方式來說……） **Let me stress again that…** （容我再度強調……） **To put it more precisely…** （更精確地說……）

❼ To show cause/effect（顯示因果關係）

General（一般用字）	Advanced alternatives（進階選擇）
Consequently…（因此……） Because…（因為……） Due to…（由於……） If this occurs, then… （若如此…… 那麼……） Since…（既然……） For that reason…（基於此原因……） As a result…（結果是……） …caused by…（也因為……） For this reason…（基於此原因……） In that case…（此情況下……） Otherwise…（否則……） Unless…（除非……）	**… is ascribed to…**（歸因於……） **Due to the fact that…**（由於……） **Thanks to…**（拜… 所賜……） **… leads to…**（導致……） **… provokes…**（引發……） **On account of…**（尤於……） **As a consequence of…**（後果是……） **In consequence of…**（後果是……）

❽ To show time relationships（顯示時間之關係）

General（一般用字）	Advanced alternatives（進階選擇）
At first...（最初……）	... to date（現今……）
Immediately...（立即……）	At present...（目前……）
Then...（接著……）	At the present stage...（現階段……）
Later...（後來……）	Currently...（目前……）
Afterwards...（隨後……）	Last but not least...（最後……）
After that...（接著……）	For now...（現今……）
Before...（之前……）	For the time being...（就目前來說……）
While...（當……）	at the same time...（同時……）
During...（在……期間……）	From time to time...（三不五時……）
As soon as...（立即……）	... every now and then...（時而……）
Sometime...（有時……）	Occasionally,（偶爾……）
Last...（最後……）	Once in a while...（時而……）
Frequently...（經常……）	
When...（當……）	
Once...（一度……）	
Oftentimes...（常常……）	
Meanwhile...（與此同時……）	
Finally...（最後……）	

❾ To show contrast（顯示對立意見）

General（一般用字）	Advanced alternatives（進階選擇）
Some people may argue that... （有些人可能會反駁……）	Whereas...（然而……）
Although...（雖說……）	Surprisingly enough... （出乎意料的……）
Even though...（雖然……）	Unfortunately...（不幸地……）

Instead… （取而代之……）

In contrast… （相對之下……）

On the one hand… on the other hand…
（一方面… 就另一方面……）

However… （但是……）

In spite of… （即使……）

Despite… （儘管……）

Unlike… （不像……）

But… （但是……）

Yet… （但是……）

Rather than… （而是……）

Either… or… （或……）

Nor… （也不……）

Neither… （兩者皆不……）

Neither… nor… （兩者皆不……）

Nevertheless… （然而……）

Nonetheless… （儘管如此……）

None… （沒有……）

While… （儘管……）

From a… perspective…
（由……角度來看……）

On the contrary… （反之……）

Beyond our imagination…
（超乎我們想像……）

Strikingly… （引人注目地……）

Instead… （取而代之……而是……）

Despite the fact that… （縱然……）

⑩ To Emphasize （強調要點）

General （一般用字）	Advanced alternatives （進階選擇）
Above all… （尤其是……）	Indeed… （的確……）
Clearly… （顯然地……）	Absolutely… （絕對地……）
Actually… （事實上……）	Positively… （肯定地……）
In fact… （實際上……）	Surprisingly… （出乎意料地……）
Certainly… （的確是……）	Without a doubt… （毫無疑問……）

Definitely... （確認是……）	**Evidently...** （明顯地……）
Extremely... （極度地……）	**Obviously...** （顯然地……）
Especially... （尤其是……）	**Mainly...** （主要地……）
I mean... （我的意思是……）	**Without exception,...** （毫無例外……）
That is to say... （也就是說……）	**The importance of... cannot be overemphasized...** （… 重要性無法被忽略……）
The key point is that... （關鍵是……）	**It is important to bear in mind that...** （要記得的是……）
	I'd like to lay special emphasis on... （我要特別強調的是……）

⑪ To choose an option over another （表明偏好）

General （一般用字）	Advanced alternatives （進階選擇）
...might be the better choice （…… 會是較佳的選擇）	**It is a mistake to think that...** （認為… 是錯的……）
...makes it a better policy （…… 是更好的方針）	**It might be an error to assume that...** （假定… 是不對的……）
It's beneficial... （……是有益的……）	**It would not make sense to think that...** （會認為… 是沒道理的……）
... is better than... （……是更好的……）	**It is pointless to argue whether...** （爭論… 是無意義的……）
... is superior to... （……比較優的……）	

⑫ To show similarity （顯示相同點）

General （一般用字）	Advanced alternatives （進階選擇）
As...as... （像……一般……）	**Similarly...** （一樣地……）
Just as... （就像……）	**Likewise...** （類似地……）
In the same way... （如同……）	

⑬ To show purpose（顯示目的）

General（一般用字）	Advanced alternatives（進階選擇）
For…（為了……） So that…（因此……）	**In order to…**（為了……） **Please note: For V-ing, [something] should be considered.**（為了……，應該要考慮……）

⑭ To give examples（舉例、提供細節）

General（一般用字）	Advanced alternatives（進階選擇）
As evidence of…（就證據看來……） Such as…（如同……） For example…（舉例來說……） For instance…（比方說……） Take myself as an example…（就我自己的例子……） A few of these are…（一些例子是……） In the case of…（在……情況下……） For one thing… for another…（一為…… 另一方面是……） … illustrated with…（顯示出……） In this case…（此狀況下……） In another case…（另一方面……） … including…（包括……） Particularly…（尤其是……） Specifically…（特別是……） To demonstrate…（證明如下……） To illustrate…（舉例來看……） … as follows…（如下所示……）	**A supporting fact is that…**（事實是……） **A sad fact is that…**（不幸地……） **A significant reason is that…**（很明顯的原因為……） **A vivid example is…**（清楚的例子是……） **An example that comes to mind is…**（我想到一個例子……） **This fact is supported by another example…**（還有另一例子可以證實此事……） **The evidence suggests…**（證據指出……） **An undeniable fact can be found…**（不可反駁的事實便是…） **… is a notable / typical example…**（……是個典型的例子……） **To take a simple example,…**（舉個簡單的例子……）

	Two examples will suffice to show… （兩個例子便足以說明⋯⋯）
	There are many cases where… （很多狀況顯示⋯⋯）
	I will give an example to illustrate… （讓我舉個例子來說明⋯⋯）

⑮ To state the Problem（描述問題點）

General（一般用字）	Advanced alternatives（進階選擇）
The problem is that...（問題在於⋯⋯） The question is...（問題是⋯⋯）	**The disadvantage is that…** （缺點是⋯⋯） **What's being challenged is that…** （挑戰點在於⋯⋯） **The question we must consider next is…**（我們接著要考量的問題是⋯⋯） **There is a further point which needs to be clarified.** （這就是要進一步確認的要點⋯⋯）

⑯ To Summarize（做結論）

General（一般用字）	Advanced alternatives（進階選擇）
Finally...（最後⋯⋯） As a result...（結果是⋯⋯） Hence...（因此⋯⋯） Therefore...（因此⋯⋯） To sum up...（總結⋯⋯） In other words...（也就是說⋯⋯）	**In sum…**（總結⋯⋯） **To summarize…**（結論是⋯⋯） **All in all…**（總而言之⋯⋯） **All things considered…**（大體而言⋯⋯） **Altogether…**（總歸一句⋯⋯） **On the whole…**（總地看來⋯⋯）

In brief... （簡言之……）

Briefly... （簡言之……）

To conclude... （總結……）

On the whole... （大抵上……）

As we have seen... （如我們所見……）

In short... （簡言之……）

To put it briefly... （簡單來說……）

It can be seen that... （由此可見……）

In the long run... （長遠來看……）

In conclusion... （結論是……）

In the end... （最後……）

We can conclude... （由此可見……）

All these explanations make it clear that... （經過解釋便可看出……）

It seems reasonable to conclude:... （由此可合理地看出……）

Simply put, （簡言之……）

To put it simply, （簡單地說……）

To make a long story short, （長話短說……）

二、現學現用句型 80 組

套用句型 ① **I'm a firm believer that [S. + V.]**

| 初級句子 | I think you can do anything you want.
我認為你可以做任何想做的事。 |

| 美化句子 | **I'm a firm believer that** you can design your own dream job.
我確信你可以設計自己的夢想職業。 |

| 舉一反三 1 | **I'm a firm believer that** all human beings are equal.
我確信所有人都生而平等。 |

| 舉一反三 2 | **I'm a firm believer that** children should learn language as early as possible.
我確信小孩應盡早學習語言。 |

| 自由發揮 🖊 | |

＊可參考訊號字類別 ①

70

套用句型 ② **Based on my observation, S. + V.**

| 初級句子 | I see that people who have many skills can succeed.
我認為擁有多個技能的人會成功。 |

| 美化句子 | **Based on my observation**, people with multiple skills are more likely to succeed.
根據我的觀察，擁有多項技能的人比較容易成功。 |

| 舉一反三 1 | **Based on my observation**, optimistic people tend to tolerate setbacks better.
根據我的觀察，樂觀的的人比較容易忍受挫折。 |

| 舉一反三 2 | **Based on my observation**, students with good organizational ability perform better at school.
根據我的觀察，有組織能力的學生在校表現會比較好。 |

| 自由發揮✐ | |

[something] depends on [factor#1, factor#2, and factor#3].

初級句子	What children will become has something to do with experiences, and other things. 小孩會變成如何跟他們的經驗與其他事情有關係。

美化句子	Children's personality development **depends on** their experiences, values, and their parents' expectations. 小孩的人格養成取決於他們的經驗、價值觀和父母的期望。

舉一反三 1	A country's prosperity **depends on** its natural resources, economic system, and its conditions in foreign trade. 一個國家的繁榮取決於其天然資源、經濟系統與國貿的狀況。

舉一反三 2	The success of small companies **depends on** product development, customer service, and their business strategy. 小企業的成功取決於產品開發、客戶服務與商業策略。

自由發揮	

＊可參考訊號字類別 ②

套用句型 4 [something] is mainly dependent upon whether [someone] can [do something].

| 初級句子 | True success is whether you finish what you want to do.
真正的成功是看你是否完成你想做的。 |

| 美化句子 | Individual success **is mainly dependent upon whether** a person **can** achieve important personal goals.
個人的成功主要是看一個人是否達成重要的個人目標而定。 |

| 舉一反三 1 | Business success **is mainly dependent upon whether** the company **can** accomplish its sales targets.
生意的成功主要是看一個公司是否達成業績目標而定。 |

| 舉一反三 2 | Long-term relationship success **is mainly dependent upon whether** the couple **can** handle conflicts in a rational manner.
長期關係的成功主要是看一對戀人是否能理性處理衝突而定。 |

| 自由發揮 ✐ | |

套用句型 ⑤ The ability to develop [something] is critical for [someone].

初級句子	A leader needs to know how to build relationships with others. 一個老闆要知道如何跟人建立關係。

美化句子	**The ability to develop** strong relationships **is critical for** a leader. 有與人建立關係的能力對老闆來說是很重要的。

舉一反三 1	**The ability to exchange** ideas through oral communication is **critical for** a student. 有透過口語溝通來與人交換意見的能力對學生來說是很重要的。

舉一反三 2	**The ability to enforce** reasonable rules **is critical for** parents. 會建立合理規範的能力對父母來說是很重要的。

自由發揮✎	

套用句型 ⑥ There are a number of ways we can [do something] more + adv.

初級句子	We do many things to save water. 我們做很多事來節省水源。

美化句子	**There are a number of ways we can** use water **more** efficiently. 有很多方式讓我們更有效地用水。

舉一反三 1	**There are a number of ways we can** figure out solutions **more** thoroughly. 有很多方式讓我們更全面地想出解決方案。

舉一反三 2	**There are a number of ways we can** improve communication skills **more** effortlessly. 有很多方式讓我們更輕易地增進溝通技巧。

自由發揮 ✏	

套用句型 ⑦ **[doing something] + impact#1 and impact#2.**

初級句子	Traveling makes us smart and more open to new things. 旅遊讓我們變聰明，也瞭解更多。

美化句子	**Traveling** increases our knowledge **and** widens our perspective. 旅遊增加我們的知識，也拓展了我們的視野。

舉一反三 1	**Reading novels** stimulates our imagination **and** expands our vocabulary. 讀小說激發了我們的想像力，也拓展了單字量。

舉一反三 2	**Exercise** helps us reduce mental stress **and** boosts happy chemicals. 運動讓我們減輕精神壓力，也讓激發腦內快樂物質的分泌。

自由發揮 ✎	

套用句型 8 **There is no greater feeling in the world than [doing something].**

初級句子	I felt the happiest after running my first marathon. 在我完成第一次馬拉松跑步後，我感到很快樂。

美化句子	**There is no greater feeling in the world than** running your first marathon. 世上沒有比跑完第一次馬拉松之後更棒的感覺了。

舉一反三 1	**There is no greater feeling in the world than** completing your first novel. 世上沒有比完成自己第一本小說之後更棒的感覺了。

舉一反三 2	**There is no greater feeling in the world than** closing your first business deal. 世上沒有比結下第一筆案子之後更棒的感覺了。

自由發揮 ✎	

S., who…, V.

初級句子	Ms. Smith is an English teacher and she says we have to read a lot of books. 史密斯小姐是一個英文老師，她說我們要多讀點書。

美化句子	Ms. Smith, **who** is our English teacher, encourages us to read as much as possible. 史密斯小姐，我們的英文老師，鼓勵我們要多閱讀。

舉一反三 1	My father, **who** works as a director, is usually too busy to spend quality time with us. 我爸爸，身為一位總裁，總是忙到沒時間陪我們。

舉一反三 2	Linda, **who** is my best friend, shares her innermost secrets with me. 琳達，也就是我的好朋友，會和我分享內心的秘密。

自由發揮✐	

套用句型 ⑩ As a [someone], he/she visualizes himself/herself as [adj.]

初級句子

Because she is a teacher, she thinks she should be confident.
因爲她是老師,她認爲她應該要有自信。

美化句子

As a teacher, she visualizes herself as calm, confident, and smiling.
身爲老師,她視自己爲沉穩、自信和面帶微笑的人。

舉一反三 1

As a sales representative, Jack visualizes himself as friendly, passionate, and cheerful.
身爲業務,傑克視自己爲友善、有熱情和愉悅的人。

舉一反三 2

As a basketball player, Mary visualizes herself as tough, skillful, and aggressive.
身爲籃球隊員,瑪莉視自己爲堅強、技巧出眾和積極的人。

自由發揮 ✎

[something] is the key to [something].

初級句子	Forgive people and you will feel happy. 原諒別人，你會感到快樂。

⇩

美化句子	Forgiveness **is the key to** happiness and inner peace. 諒解是快樂和內心平靜的關鍵。

舉一反三 1	Diligence **is the key to** well-being and success. 勤奮是幸福和成功的關鍵。

舉一反三 2	Persistence **is the key to** triumph and satisfaction. 堅持是成功和滿足的關鍵。

自由發揮 ✐	

套用句型 ⑫ **If I could invent a new product, I would develop / design / devise [something].**

初級句子	If I wanted to make a new product, it would be a machine to read people's minds. 若我要發明新產品，會是可以讀心思的機器。

美化句子	**If I could invent a new product, I would develop** a mind-reading machine. 若我可以發明新產品，我會想發明讀心機。

舉一反三 1	**If I could invent a new product, I would design** an automatic translator. 若我可以發明新產品，我會想發明自動翻譯機。

舉一反三 2	**If I could invent a new product, I would devise** a flying boat. 若我可以發明新產品，我會想發明會飛的船。

自由發揮✐	

＊可參考訊號字類別 ③

套用句型 ⑬ If [someone] want(s) to [do something], [someone] will / should / can / may / must...

初級句子	If you want to win, you have to work hard. 若你想要贏，你就要努力工作。

美化句子	**If you want to** get one-up on others, **you must** work your tail off. 若你想略勝他人一籌，你必須全力以赴。

舉一反三 1	**If we want to** make the world a better place to live in, **we should** conserve the environment. 若人們想要讓世界變成一個更適合居住的地方，大家就要保育環境。

舉一反三 2	**If a sales representative wants to** close more deals, **he can** make more cold calls. 若一個業務想結下更多案子，那他就要多打些電話開發客戶。

自由發揮 ✎	

＊可參考訊號字類別 ③

套用句型 ⑭ If + S. + V-ed..., S. + would / could / might + V....

初級句子

We couldn't arrange marketing activities, because we didn't have enough money.

我們沒辦行銷活動，因為我們沒足夠的錢。

美化句子

If we had sufficient budget, we **could** arrange more marketing campaigns.

若我們有足夠的預算，我們就可以安排更多行銷活動。

舉一反三 1

If there wasn't so much red tape, my company **would** be up and running already.

若非有這麼多繁文縟節，我公司早就上軌道營運了。

舉一反三 2

If there were room for me to advance in the company, I **might** stay for another two years.

若在此公司還有管道讓我升遷的話，我會再待兩年。

自由發揮 ✎

＊可參考訊號字類別 ③

套用句型 ⑮ **If + S. + had + p.p., S. + would / should / could / might + have + p.p.…**

初級句子	I felt ill for a long time, because I didn't listen to the doctor and take the medicine. 我的病拖很久沒好，因為我沒按醫生的吩咐吃藥。

美化句子	**If I had** listened to the doctor and taken the medicine, **I might have** got better sooner. 要是我有聽醫生的話吃藥，我的病應該早就好了。

舉一反三 1	**If I had** established my own business ten years ago, **I might have** become a millionaire much sooner. 要是我十年前就自己創業的話，我可能會更快速致富。

舉一反三 2	**If I had** studied harder, **I would have** passed the exam. 若我努力點唸書的話，我早該通過考試了。

自由發揮 ✎	

＊可參考訊號字類別 ③

套用句型 ⑯ S + hope that + S can + V /will be able to + V/V.
未來時間副詞

| 初級句子 | I hope to be the Head of Engineering next year.
我希望明年可以當工程部經理。 |

| 美化句子 | I **hope that** I **can** be promoted as Head of Engineering next year.
我希望明年我可以升官成為工程部經理。 |

| 舉一反三 1 | I **hope that** I **will be able to** complete this project by next Friday.
我希望本週五前我可以完成此專案。 |

| 舉一反三 2 | I **hope that** I **find** a proper solution to this problem soon.
我希望很快地可以找到此問題的解決方案。 |

| 自由發揮✎ | |

套用句型 ⑰ **Research shows that not only [V. + S. …], but [S. + V. …]**

初級句子	Research shows that taking vacations is good for us, and taking vacations can help us have more energy too. 研究指出渡假對我們是有益的，渡假也可以讓我們有活力。

美化句子	**Research shows that not only** are vacations good for our mind, **but** they can also help us boost energy. 研究指出渡假不僅對我們的心靈有益處，也可以增進我們的活力。

舉一反三 **1**	**Research shows that not only** can reading novels sharpen our imagination, **but** it can also expand the scope of our knowledge. 研究指出讀小說不僅讓我們有敏銳的想像力，也可以拓展知識。

舉一反三 **2**	**Research shows that not only** can exercise increase our metabolic rate, **but** it can also increase physical strength. 研究指出運動不僅可以增加新陳代謝力，也可能增加我們的力量。

自由發揮 ✐	

＊可參考訊號字類別 ④

套用句型 ⑱ **[something] is not the only [something] that [something] can offer.**

初級句子	The Internet offers information, and more things. 網路提供資訊，和更多東西。

美化句子	Information **is not the only** advantage that the Internet **can offer**. 網路的優點可不只提供資訊而已。

舉一反三 1	Insurance **is not the only** benefit that the company **can offer**. 公司的福利可不僅包括保險而已。

舉一反三 2	A sense of security **is not the only** function that a family **can offer**. 家庭的功能可不僅提供安全感而已。

自由發揮✎	

More [something] can be found in [somewhere].

| 初級句子 | You can find more related books in the library.
你可以在圖書館找到更多參考書。 |

| 美化句子 | **More** reference books **can be found in** the Science Section in the library.
更多參考書可以在圖書館內的科學區被找到。 |

| 舉一反三 1 | **More** explanations **can be found in** the files available on the company intranet.
更多的解釋可以在公司內部網路的檔案內找到。 |

| 舉一反三 2 | **More** examples **can be found in** encyclopedias.
更多的例子可以在百科全書內被找到。 |

| 自由發揮 🖉 | |

＊可參考訊號字類別 ④

套用句型 20 **This example is sufficient to show + S. + V....**

初級句子	From this example, we can see that we need to work hard in order to succeed. 從此例子可以看出，我們要成功就要努力工作。

美化句子	**This example is sufficient to show** that hard-work can produce real results. 此例子足以證明，勤奮可以帶來真正的成就。

舉一反三 1	**This example is sufficient to show** that success is a competition with ourselves. 此例子足以證明，成功是一場與自己的比賽。

舉一反三 2	**This example is sufficient to show** that people gain respect from devoting 100% effort to their work. 此例子足以證明，人們受到的尊敬來自於奉獻全力的精神。

自由發揮 🖉	

套用句型 ㉑ [something] is essential for [something.]

初級句子	MRT is very important for a city's development. 捷運對一個都市的發展是很重要的。

美化句子	A well-developed public transportation system **is essential for** the prosperity of a society. 一個完善的公共運輸系統對社會的繁榮是很重要的。

舉一反三 1	Strong financial backup **is essential for** the success of a company. 強力的財務後盾對一個公司的成敗是很重要的。

舉一反三 2	Excellent communication skills **are essential for** the development of a relationship. 良好的溝通對一段關係的發展是很重要的。

自由發揮 🖊	

＊可參考訊號字類別 ④

套用句型 ㉒ [somewhere] is famous for its [something…]

初級句子	Taipei has business center. Taipei has pubs. Taipei has night-markets. 台北有商業中心、台北有酒吧、台北有夜市。

美化句子	Taipei **is famous for its** bustling business centers, energetic nightlife, and colorful marketplaces. 台北以熙攘的商業中心、活力夜生活和多彩的商場著名。

舉一反三 1	Japan **is famous for its** blossom trees, traditional temples, and fantastic Mount Fuji. 日本以生長茂盛的樹木、傳統的廟宇和令人驚嘆的富士山著稱。

舉一反三 2	Brazil **is famous for its** amazing beaches, various festivals, and amazing Amazon rainforests. 巴西以精彩的海灘、各式節慶和令人驚豔的亞馬遜雨林著稱。

自由發揮 ✎	

套用句型 ㉓ **[something] is / are important characteristic(s) of [something].**

初級句子	To keep healthy relationships, we have to have empathy. 為保持良好關係，我們要有同理心。

美化句子	Empathy **is** one of the most **important characteristics of** healthy relationships. 同理心在良好關係中是很重要的一個特性。

舉一反三 1	Organization and clarity **are** two **important characteristics of** effective teachers. 組織能力和講解清晰對好老師來說是兩個重要的特性。

舉一反三 2	Passion and motivation **are** two **essential characteristics of** successful entrepreneurs. 熱情和動機對成功創業家來說是兩個重要的特性。

自由發揮🖉	

套用句型 24 ... both [A] and [B]...

| 初級句子 | People are eating more food, so they are becoming fat.
人們越吃越多，因此也越來越胖。 |

| 美化句子 | Nowadays people are gaining **both** appetite **and** weight.
現在人們的胃口和體重都同時增加了。 |

| 舉一反三 1 | Practicing yoga helps people increase strength **both** physically **and** mentally.
練習瑜伽讓人們同時增加身體與心靈上的力量。 |

| 舉一反三 2 | After the long journey, the passengers were **both** exhausted **and** starving.
在長途旅行之後，旅客都又累又餓了。 |

| 自由發揮 ✎ | |

*可參考訊號字類別 ④

套用句型 25 **The best way to [do something] is by [something].**

初級句子	If I want to improve my English, I need to practice more. 若我想讓英文進步，我要多練習。

美化句子	**The best way to** sharpen my English **is by** ongoing practice. 要精進英文最佳的方式是透過持續的練習。

舉一反三 1	**The best way to** generate more sales leads **is by** adequate marketing campaigns. 要產生更多客戶名單的方式是透過有效的行銷活動。

舉一反三 2	**The best way to** score high on exams **is by** effective preparation. 要提高考試分數的最佳方式是透過有效的準備。

自由發揮 ✎	

Nowadays [someone] be addicted to [doing something]

初級句子	Nowadays people use Facebook a lot. 現在大家都使用臉書。

⇩

美化句子	**Nowadays** people **are addicted to** using social network platforms. 現在人們沉溺於使用社交平台。

舉一反三 1	**Nowadays** young people **are addicted to** playing online games. 現在年輕人沉溺於玩線上遊戲。

舉一反三 2	**Nowadays** some women **are addicted to** getting plastic surgery. 現在有些女人沉溺於做整形手術。

自由發揮 ✐	

The assumption / fact / concept that [S. + V.] is now widely accepted.

初級句子

People now believe that global warming changes weather conditions.

人們現在相信全球氣溫升高改變了氣候狀況。

美化句子

The assumption that global warming has made climate more extreme **is now widely accepted**.

全球氣溫升高會改變氣候狀況的推測現在已被廣為接受了。

舉一反三 1

The fact that human brains are different **is now widely accepted**.

人類的腦都長得不一樣的事實現在已被廣為接受了。

舉一反三 2

The concept that citizens are equal under the law **is now widely accepted**.

法律之前人人平等的概念現在已被廣為接受了。

自由發揮 🖉

套用句型 28 [someone] always remind [someone] to [do something].

初級句子	My parents always ask me to be myself. 我父母總是叫我要做自己。

美化句子	My parents **always remind** me **to** be honest about who I am. 我父母總是提醒我要忠於自己。

舉一反三 1	The teacher **always reminds** her students not **to** live to someone else's expectations. 老師總是提醒同學不要活在別人的期待中。

舉一反三 2	His supervisor **always reminds** him **to** stand out from the crowd. 他老闆總是提醒他要與眾不同。

自由發揮 🖉	

套用句型 ㉙ In other words, [something] is vital.

| 初級句子 | So it is very important to prepare first.
因此,事先準備是很重要的。 |

| 美化句子 | **In other words**, advance preparation **is vital**.
換言之,事前準備是關鍵。 |

| 舉一反三 1 | **In other words**, effective communication **is vital**.
換言之,有效的溝通是關鍵。 |

| 舉一反三 2 | **In other words**, careful risk management **is vital**.
換言之,仔細的風險管理是關鍵。 |

| 自由發揮✐ | |

＊可參考訊號字類別 ⑥

套用句型 30 I make an effort to [do something] so that I'm /will be/ able to [do something.]

初級句子	I try hard to spend equal time between office and home, and then I can enjoy my own life. 我儘量做到工作和家庭平衡，以便享受自己的生活。

美化句子	**I make an effort to** keep my work-life balance at a very comfortable level **so that I'm able to** enjoy all areas of my life. 我儘量在工作和家庭之間取得適當的平衡，以便享受生命的各種層面。

舉一反三 1	**Mr. Jones makes an effort to** accumulate as much wealth as possible **so that he'll be able to** enjoy his retirement. 瓊斯先生儘量累積財富，以便以後可享受退休生活。

舉一反三 2	**She makes an effort to** perfect her English skills **so that she'll be able to** conduct her presentation in English without difficulties. 她盡力地加強英文能力，以便可以毫無困難地用英文做簡報。

自由發揮 🖉	

套用句型 31 [someone's trait] has won him / her complete [something] from [someone].

初級句子	Mr. Jones is very honest, so his business partners respect him. 瓊斯先生很誠實，所以他的業務夥伴都尊敬他。

美化句子	Mr. Jones's integrity **has won him complete** respect **from** his business partners. 瓊斯先生的誠信讓他贏得了業務夥伴的尊敬。

舉一反三 1	Sandra's kindness **has won her complete** appreciation **from** her friends. 珊卓的善心讓她贏得了朋友的感謝。

舉一反三 2	Jack's diligent attitude **has won him complete** recognition **from** the management. 傑克的勤奮態度讓他贏得了管理階級的注意。

自由發揮 ✐	

套用句型 ③2 **[something] is an essential tool that [someone] depend on for [something].**

初級句子	The Internet is very popular. People have to use the Internet to communicate. 網路很普遍。人們都透過網路溝通。

美化句子	The Internet **is an essential tool that** people **depend** heavily **on for** daily communication. 網路是相當普遍的工具，人們重度依賴網路做日常溝通。

舉一反三 1	Microsoft Office package **is an essential tool that** students **depend** heavily **on for** report editing. 微軟的 Office 軟體已是很普遍的工具，學生重度依賴此軟體來修改報告。

舉一反三 2	Java **is an essential tool that** software designers **depend** heavily **on for** program coding. Java 是很普遍的工具，軟體設計師重度依賴它來編寫程式。

自由發揮✎	

套用句型 ③ Thanks to [something], [S. + V.]

初級句子	The weather was good, so we had a good trip to Japan. 天氣很好，所以我們的日本之旅很好玩。

美化句子	**Thanks to** the wonderful weather, our journey to Japan was comfortable. 拜好天氣所賜，我們的日本之旅很舒適。

舉一反三 1	**Thanks to** the public transportation system, Taipei has become a center of business and technology development. 拜公共運輸系統所賜，台北已變成商業和科技發展中心。

舉一反三 2	**Thanks to** technological advances, solar power is about to become more economical. 拜科技進步所賜，太陽能已快變得更便宜了。

自由發揮 🖉	

＊可參考訊號字類別 ⑦

The [something] gap might lead to [something].

初級句子	A big age difference makes people think differently. 年紀的差異讓人們想法不同。

⇩

美化句子	**The generation gap might lead to** misunderstandings. 年齡的差距會導致誤解。

舉一反三 1	**The wealth gap might lead to** a higher level of poverty. 貧富的差距會導致更多的貧窮。

舉一反三 2	**The expectation gap might lead to** frustration. 期待的差距會導致失望。

自由發揮	

套用句型 ③⑤ [doing something] enables [someone] to [do something].

初級句子	If you have more than one skill, you will have more opportunities. 若你擁有一項以上的專長，你就有較多的機會。

美化句子	Obtaining multiple skills **enables** people **to** expand their opportunities. 擁有多樣專長讓人能夠拓展更多機會。

舉一反三 1	Studying abroad alone **enables** students **to** stretch their comfort zones. 獨立出國留學讓學生能夠拓展他們的舒適圈。

舉一反三 2	Participating in brainstorm meetings **enables** specialists **to** come up with more creative ideas. 參與腦力激盪的會議讓專員可以想出更多有創意的點子。

自由發揮 ✎	

套用句型 36 [something] has caused a revolution in our way of [something].

| 初級句子 | The Internet has brought people a new way to communicate.
網路帶給人們新的溝通方式。 |

| 美化句子 | The Internet **has caused a revolution in our way of** communication.
網路為人們帶來革命性的溝通方式。 |

| 舉一反三 1 | The well-developed MRT system in Taipei **has caused a revolution in people's way of** commuting.
台北完善的捷運系統為人們帶來革命性的通勤方式。 |

| 舉一反三 2 | The invention of jets **has caused a revolution in our way of** traveling.
客機的發明為人類帶來革命性的旅遊方式。 |

| 自由發揮 ✎ | |

always associate [A] with [B].

初級句子	Whenever I see storybooks, I think of my mother. 每當我看到故事書，就想到我媽媽。

美化句子	I **always associate** storybooks **with** my mother. 我總是把故事書和媽媽聯想在一起。

舉一反三 1	People **always associate** rainy days **with** depression. 人們總是把下雨天和憂鬱聯想在一起。

舉一反三 2	She **always associates** the smell of cookies **with** her grandmother. 她總是把餅乾的香味和外婆聯想在一起。

自由發揮 ✐	

套用句型 38 In recent years, [some group of people] have taken a closer look at [something] and how it might [influence].

初級句子	Recently, scientists have been studying jogging more and are beginning to see the relation to people's health. 最近，科學家對慢跑的研究更多了，並找到與人體健康的關係。

美化句子	**In recent years, scientists have taken a closer look at** jogging **and how it might** improve people's muscle strength. 近幾年，科學家更深入地研究慢跑，和慢跑是如何幫助人們增進肌肉強度。

舉一反三 1	**In recent years, researchers have taken a closer look at** meditation **and how it might** improve people's concentration. 近幾年，研究人員更深入地研究冥想，和冥想是如何增進人們的精神狀態。

舉一反三 2	**In recent years, doctors have taken a closer look at** smoking **and how it might** be associated with cancers. 近幾年，醫生家更深入地研究吸煙，和吸煙與癌症間的關係。

自由發揮 ✐	

[someone] spends [time] [doing something] first thing in the morning.

初級句子	At the beginning of every day, Mr. Jones always reads. 在一天的開始，瓊斯先生總會先看書。

美化句子	Mr. Jones **spends** at least one hour reading **first thing in the morning**. 瓊斯先生每天第一件事是花至少一小時讀書。

舉一反三 1	Linda **spends** at least thirty minutes checking emails **first thing in the morning**. 琳達每天第一件事是花至少三十分鐘看電子郵件。

舉一反三 2	I **spend** at least two hours practicing yoga **first thing in the morning**. 我每天第一件事是花至少兩小時練習瑜伽。

自由發揮 🖉	

套用句型 40 **[something] available to [someone] has increased dramatically.**

初級句子	There are many new devices we can use today. 現在有很多我們可以用的新設備。

美化句子	The technological apparatus **available to** today's presenters **has increased dramatically**. 現在簡報者可以利用的科技設備大量增加。

舉一反三 1	The number of online encyclopedias **available to** today's students **has increased dramatically**. 現在學生可以利用的線上百科全書大量增加。

舉一反三 2	The number of analytical applications **available to** today's workers **has increased dramatically**. 現在上班族可以利用的分析應用程式大量增加。

自由發揮 ✎	

[someone] used to believe that [S. + V.], but now they know that [S. + V.]

初級句子	Scientists said that the brain didn't do anything while sleeping, but now they know they were wrong. 科學家以前說人腦在睡眠時沒有在運作，但現在他們知道他們錯了。

美化句子	Scientists **used to believe that** the brain was inactive during sleep, **but now they know that** this is not the case. 科學家一度認為在睡眠中人腦沒有運作，但現在他們發覺並非如此。

舉一反三 1	Parents **used to think that** children were not learning anything when playing, **but now they know that** this is not true. 父母一度認為小孩在玩耍時便沒在學習，但現在他們知道事實不是這樣。

舉一反三 2	Manufacturers **used to consider that** consumers only liked cheaper products, **but now they understand this** is halfway correct. 廠商一度認為客戶只喜歡便宜的商品，但現在他們瞭解那並不全然正確。

自由發揮 🖉	

套用句型 ㊷ Just because [S. + V.] doesn't mean [someone] can't [do something].

初級句子	I'm taking a vacation, but why can't I read my favorite book? 我要去渡假，就不能帶我最喜歡的書嗎？

美化句子	**Just because** I'm going on a vacation **doesn't mean** I **can't** take my favorite book with me. 就因為我是要去渡假，不代表我就不能帶最喜歡的書去看吧。

舉一反三 1	**Just because** they travel to Japan for business purposes **doesn't mean** they **can't** go sightseeing and relax a bit. 就只是因為他們去日本是為了公事，不代表他們就不能看風景輕鬆一下吧。

舉一反三 2	**Just because** students are supposed to study hard **doesn't mean** they **can't** hang out with friends during the weekend. 就只是因為學生應該要認真唸書，不代表他們在週末不能跟同學出去玩吧。

自由發揮 ✐	

S. + V....; however, S. +V....

初級句子	The service will cost a lot. But it's worth it. 那服務很貴。但有其價值。

美化句子	The solution will be really costly; **however**, it's worth it. 那套解決方案真的很昂貴,但值得。

舉一反三 1	Losing the competition doesn't really matter to Linda; **however**, John can't stand it. 琳達對輸掉比賽不是很在意,但是,約翰就無法忍受了。

舉一反三 2	All team members tried the best; **however**, we eventually lost the case. 所有同仁都盡力了,但是,我們還是輸掉了案子。

自由發揮 ✐	

＊可參考訊號字類別 ⑨

套用句型 ④④ [some people] may argue that S. + V....

初級句子	Other people doing business may say that people respect them because of money. 其他做生意的人可能會說，大家尊敬他們是因為錢的關係。

美化句子	Some businessmen **may argue that** people respect them simply because they possess huge sum of money. 一些生意人可能會反駁，認為大家尊敬他們純粹是因此他們擁有財富。

舉一反三 1	Some psychologists **may argue that** children should learn to use modern technological devices as early as possible. 一些反對者可能會反駁，認為小孩學習使用現代科技裝置要越早越好。

舉一反三 2	Some naysayers **may argue that** by working at home, workers can save on hidden costs associated with commuting. 一些唱反調的人可能會反駁，認為在家工作可以省下通勤的相關費用。

自由發揮✎	

＊可參考訊號字類別 ⑨

[doing something] is a dream for many people, but in fact it has its pitfalls / disadvantages / downsides / drawbacks.

初級句子	People like to work at home, but it is not without problems. 人們喜歡在家工作，但那也並非是沒問題的。

美化句子	Working at home **is a dream for many workers, but in fact it has its pitfalls.** 在家工作是很多上班族的夢想，但事實上也有其缺點。

舉一反三 1	Being a freelance worker **is a dream for many people, but in fact it has its disadvantages.** 當自由工作者是很多人的夢想，但事實上也是有其缺點。

舉一反三 2	Winning big in the lottery **is a dream for many people, but in fact it has its downsides.** 贏得大筆樂透獎金是很多人的夢想，但事實上也是有其缺點。

自由發揮 ✎	

套用句型 46 Not only [V. + S.], but [S.] also [V.]...（前句倒裝）/ [S.] not only [V.]..., but [S.] also [V.]...

初級句子	Good supervisors should know what their workers can do. They also need to set goals. 好的老闆要知道員工的能力，他們也要設立目標。

美化句子	**Not only** do good supervisors understand team members' potential, **but** they **also** set achievable goals. 好的老闆不僅要瞭解員工的潛能，也要設定可達成的目標。

舉一反三 1	A seasoned supervisor **not only** motivates employees to perform professionally, **but** he **also** urges members to welcome new challenges. 一個有經驗的老闆不僅會激勵員工專業任職，也會鼓勵員工勇於面對新挑戰。

舉一反三 2	Helping with household chores **not only** fosters children's household skills, **but** it **also** enables them to develop a sense of responsibility. 協助做家事不僅能培養小孩的家務技巧，也可讓他們學習到責任感。

自由發揮✐	

＊可參考訊號字類別 ④

套用句型 47 I'd like to stress / highlight / emphasize that we each share responsibility for [something].

初級句子	I want to say that each of us has the responsibility to save water. 我想說我們每個人都有責任保育水源。

美化句子	**I'd like to stress that we each share responsibility for** the sustainable management of our water resources. 我要強調，我們每個人對水資源的保育管理都有責任。

舉一反三 1	**I'd like to highlight that we each share responsibility for** the success of the company. 我要強調，我們每個人對公司的成敗都有責任。

舉一反三 2	**I'd like to emphasize that we each share responsibility for** the prosperity of society. 我要強調，我們每個人對社會繁榮都有責任。

自由發揮 ✐	

＊可參考訊號字類別 ⑩

套用句型 48 One essential / crucial / important point to consider here is whether [S. + V.].

初級句子	We need to think first whether we have enough money. 我們要先考慮是否有足夠的錢。

美化句子	**One essential point to consider here is whether** we have sufficient budget. 要考慮的要點是我們是否有足夠的預算。

舉一反三 1	**One crucial point to consider here is whether** we can meet customer demand. 要考慮的要點是我們是否可以滿足客戶的需求。

舉一反三 2	**One important point to consider here is whether** we can close more deals. 要考慮的要點是我們是否可以結更多案子。

自由發揮 ✐	

The importance of [something] cannot be overemphasized.

初級句子	Protecting the environment is very important. 保護環境是很重要的。

美化句子	**The importance of** protecting the environment **cannot be overemphasized.** 保護環境的重要性自然需要一再強調。

舉一反三 1	**The importance of** conserving natural resources **cannot be overemphasized.** 保育天然資源的重要性自然需要一再強調。

舉一反三 2	**The importance of** maintaining excellent relationships with customers **cannot be overemphasized.** 與客戶保持良好關係的重要性自然須要一再強調。

自由發揮✎	

＊可參考訊號字類別 ⑩

套用句型 50 Only by [doing something] + can + S. + V....

初級句子	If we want to close the deal, we need to provide good products. 如果我們想結案，我們要提供優質產品。

美化句子	**Only by** providing high quality products and services **can** we win this business deal. 只有透過提供優質產品和服務，我們才會贏得訂單。

舉一反三 1	**Only by** working diligently **can** people achieve their goals. 只有透過勤奮地工作才可讓人達成目標。

舉一反三 2	**Only by** practicing every day **can** you improve your English skills. 只有透過每天練習，才能讓你的英文精進。

自由發揮 ✎	

初級句子	He had some savings so he was able to pay his bills until he found a new job. 他有些存款，因此在他找到新工作之前他有能力付帳單。

美化句子	**It was** his previous savings **that** helped him meet his financial obligations until he got back on his feet. 就是他原有的存款，讓他在重新振作起來之前有能力支付費用。

舉一反三 1	**It was** Jack's effective strategy **that** saved the whole team. 就是傑克的有效策略，救了整個團隊。

舉一反三 2	**It was** the terrible weather conditions **that** caused the flight delays. 就是天氣很糟之故，才讓班機都延誤了。

自由發揮✎	

套用句型 52 **[something] makes me realize the importance of [something].**

初級句子	After this experience, I know it is very important to save money. 有了這經驗之後，我知道存錢是很重要的。

美化句子	This experience **makes me realize the importance of** saving money for a rainy day. 此次經驗讓我瞭解到未雨綢繆的重要性。

舉一反三 1	This incident **makes me realize the importance of** collaborating with colleagues. 此事件讓我瞭解到與同事合作的重要性。

舉一反三 2	This project **makes me realize the importance of** budget management. 此專案讓我瞭解到預算規劃的重要性。

自由發揮 🖉	

套用句型 53 **[something] plays a(n) significant / essential / vital role in [something].**

初級句子	If we want to succeed, we have to have intelligence and imagination. 若我們想成功,我們要有才智和想像力。

美化句子	Intelligence and imagination **play significant roles in** success. 才智與想像力在成功的道路上扮演重要的角色。

舉一反三 1	Creativity **plays an essential role in** a fulfilling life. 創造力在滿足人生的道路上扮演重要的角色。

舉一反三 2	Personal growth **plays a vital role in** a satisfying career. 個人成長在滿意的職涯上扮演重要的角色。

自由發揮 ✏	

套用句型 54 The more / less（比較級）..., the more / worse（比較級）...

| 初級句子 | If you make fewer mistakes, you will get higher score.
你少犯點錯，你就會得高分。 |

| 美化句子 | **The fewer** mistakes you make, **the higher** your score is.
你犯的錯越少，分數就越高。 |

| 舉一反三 1 | **The more** you feel anger, **the greater** the hurt becomes.
你越感覺生氣，所造成的傷害就越大。 |

| 舉一反三 2 | **The more** I think about this, **the more** sense it makes.
我越想越覺得有道理。 |

| 自由發揮 ✎ | |

套用句型 55 **I prefer to [do A] rather than [do B]. =I prefer [doing A] to [doing B]. = I would [do A] rather than [do B]. = I would rather [do A] than [do B].**

初級句子	I want to do it myself, I don't want to ask my parents to help me. 我想靠自己的力量，不想叫父母幫我。

美化句子	**I prefer to** depend on my own ability to solve problems **rather than** ask my parents for assistance. 我寧願靠自己的能力解決問題，而非要父母出手協助。

舉一反三 1	**I would rather** study for my Master's degree abroad **than** study here at home. 我較希望到國外唸碩士，而非在國內唸書。

舉一反三 2	**I prefer** visiting customers **to** staying in the office all day. 我選擇外出拜訪客戶，而非整天待在辦公室。

自由發揮 ✎	

套用句型 56 **[to do / doing something] is one of my goals / objectives.**

| 初級句子 | I want to be a boss in the future.
我以後想當老闆。 |

⇩

| 美化句子 | Being a team leader **is one of my** long-term **objectives**.
當老闆是我的長遠目標之一。 |

| 舉一反三 1 | Studying English in the US **is one of my goals** in life.
去美國學英文是我的人生目標之一。 |

| 舉一反三 2 | Learning to windsurf **is my short-term goal** for this summer.
學衝浪是我今年暑假的短期目標。 |

| 自由發揮 ✎ | |

套用句型 57 **Some people spend [time] focusing on / doing [something].**

初級句子	Some people like to use Sunday to do many things. 有些人喜歡利用週日來完成很多事。

美化句子	**Some people spend** Sunday **focusing on** reflection, planning, and getting ready for next week. 有些人利用週日專注在回想、規劃和為下一週做準備。

舉一反三 1	**Some young people spend** Summer relaxing, socializing, and preparing for the next term. 有些年輕人利用夏天專注在放鬆、社交和為下一學期做準備。

舉一反三 2	**Some seniors spend** the weekend **focusing on** exercise, sleep, and recharging their batteries. 有些年長者利用週末專注在運動、補眠和補充體力。

自由發揮🖉	

套用句型 58 [someone] pursue / seek / crave / chase / go after [something].

| 初級句子 | Businessmen always want to make more money.
商人總是想賺更多錢。 |

⇩

| 美化句子 | Businessmen **pursue** significant wealth.
商人追求大量財富。 |

| 舉一反三 1 | Students **seek** learning.
學生追求知識。 |

| 舉一反三 2 | Human beings **crave** attention.
人類渴望關愛。 |

| 自由發揮 ✎ | |

I was impressed by / with [something].

初級句子	I liked her speech very much. 我非常喜歡她的演講。

⇩

美化句子	**I was completely impressed by** her outstanding speech. 我對她傑出的演講印象極為深刻。

舉一反三 1	**I was totally impressed with** the quality of the photos you took. 我對你所拍的照片品質印象非常深刻。

舉一反三 2	**I was really impressed by** her stunning beauty. 我對她的美貌印象非常深刻。

自由發揮 ✎	

套用句型 60 **My passion for [something] has motivated / inspired / stimulated me to choose [job] as my future career.**

初級句子	I like computers very much so I want to write programs in the future. 我很喜歡電腦，所以我以後想寫程式。

美化句子	**My passion for** computers **has motivated me to choose** software programming **as my future career.** 我對電腦的熱情促使我選擇軟體設計師為今後的職業。

舉一反三 1	**My passion for** children **has inspired me to choose** education **as my future career.** 我對小孩的熱情促使我選擇教職為今後的志業。

舉一反三 2	**My passion for** helping others **has stimulated me to choose** social work **as my future career.** 我對幫助別人的熱情促使我選擇當社會工作者為今後的職業。

自由發揮 ✎	

套用句型 61 Spending money on [something] is worthwhile, but [doing something] is equally essential.

| 初級句子 | When traveling, you need to spend some money. But you also need to save some money for the future.
旅遊時，我們要花點錢。但我們也要存點錢未來使用。 |

| 美化句子 | Spending money on traveling is worthwhile, but saving money for a rainy day is equally essential.
花點錢旅遊是值得的，存錢未雨綢繆也是相等重要。 |

| 舉一反三 1 | Spending money on hiring teachers is worthwhile, but allocating budget to improve facilities is equally essential.
花錢請老師是值得的，分配點預算升級設備也是同等重要。 |

| 舉一反三 2 | Spending money on deploying new systems is worthwhile, but distributing funds for employee training is equally essential.
花錢部署系統是值得的，分配資金做員工訓練也是同等重要。 |

| 自由發揮 ✎ | |

套用句型 62 [someone] + [do / does / did something] and ask / encourage / invite [someone] to do likewise.

| 初級句子 | Mr. Jones gave some money to the poor and asked others to follow him.
瓊斯先生捐了些錢給窮人，並叫其他人也學他。 |

| 美化句子 | Mr. Jones donated money to charities **and invited** other members **to do likewise**.
瓊斯先生捐款給慈善機構，並邀請其他員工也跟進。 |

| 舉一反三 1 | Jenny studied very hard **and urged** her young brother **to do likewise**.
珍妮很認真唸書，並督促弟弟也照做。 |

| 舉一反三 2 | Mr. and Mrs. Smith always think positively **and encourage** their children **to do likewise**.
史密斯夫婦總是正向思考，並鼓勵他們的孩子也這麼做。 |

| 自由發揮 🖋 | |

套用句型 63 **... (not) as + Adj. + as...**

初級句子	Nowadays people read less than people in the past. 現在的人們比以往少看書了。

美化句子	Nowadays people don't read **as** much **as** they did in the past. 現在的人跟過去比，相對比較不看書了。

舉一反三 1	The climate of Taiwan is **as** humid **as** that of Thailand. 台灣的氣候跟泰國的氣候一樣潮溼。

舉一反三 2	Jack's ideas are **as** creative **as** Mary's. 傑克的點子跟瑪莉的點子一樣有創意。

自由發揮✎	

*可參考訊號字類別 ⑫

套用句型 64 …by the same token…

初級句子	Some people like Hank, but others don't like him. 有些人喜歡漢克，但也有些人不喜歡他。

美化句子	Some team members think Hank is a real charmer, but **by the same token** others can't stand his behavior. 一些同仁認爲漢克是個有魅力的人，但同樣地，也有人無法忍受他的行爲。

舉一反三 1	John has a talent as a musician and **by the same token** has a sharp imagination. 約翰有音樂的天份，同樣地，他也有敏銳的想像力。

舉一反三 2	Some public figures enjoy fame, but **by the same token** they treasure their privacy. 一些公眾人物享有盛名，但同樣的，他們也注重隱私。

自由發揮 ✎	

＊可參考訊號字類別 ⑫

套用句型 65 In order to [do something], [someone] should concentrate on [doing something].

初級句子	To make more money, companies should provide what customers want. 為了要賺更多錢，公司要提供客戶所需要的。

美化句子	**In order to** be more profitable, companies **should concentrate on** fulfilling customers' needs. 為了得到更多獲利，公司應專注於滿足客戶的需求。

舉一反三 1	**In order to** perform well at school, students **should concentrate on** reviewing lessons properly. 為了在校有好表現，學生應專注在確實地複習課業。

舉一反三 2	**In order to** achieve more in life, people **should concentrate on** upgrading their skills. 為了在人生中完成更多事，人們應專注在提升能力。

自由發揮 ✐	

套用句型 66 **[someone] are encouraged to reach out to [someone] to seek [something].**

初級句子

Students should ask experienced adults for advice.
學生要向有經驗的大人請教意見。

美化句子

Students **are encouraged to reach out to** seniors with more experience **to seek** advice.
學生被鼓勵多跟有經驗的長者接觸，以聽取忠告。

舉一反三 1

Employees **are encouraged to reach out to** mentors with extensive networks **to seek** suggestions.
員工最好跟有人脈關係的良師接觸，以聽取有幫助的建言。

舉一反三 2

Sales representatives **are encouraged to reach out to** customers **to seek** constructive feedback.
業務代表最好多跟客戶接觸，以聽取有建設性的回饋意見。

自由發揮✎

套用句型 67 **[doing something] is a way of improving [something].**

初級句子

I want to improve my presentation skills, so I need to work on my body language.

我想要加強簡報能力，所以要練習肢體語言。

美化句子

Working on body language **is a way of improving** presentations.

多練習肢體語言是增進個人簡報風格的方式。

舉一反三 1

Talking to native speakers **is a way of improving** your English.

多與外國人交談會是增進你英文能力的方式。

舉一反三 2

Minimizing interruptions **is a way of improving** productivity in the workplace.

減少處理中途插進來的事件會是一個增加工作生產力的方式。

自由發揮 ✎

I will use [example/story/evidence/figures] to [illustrate/support/clarify] my point.

初級句子	I want to use an example to prove I am right. 我想用一個例子證明我是對的。

⇩

美化句子	**I will use an example to support my idea.** 我將用一個實例來支持我的看法。

舉一反三 1	**I will use evidence to support my assumption.** 我會用證據來確認我的臆測。

舉一反三 2	**I will use a real story to illustrate my point.** 我要用一個真實的故事來說明我的觀點。

自由發揮 ✎	

套用句型 69 **…, such as A, B, and other [Adj. + N.]**

初級句子	I share information on different web tools, such as Facebook, Twitter, Skype… and things like that. 我在各種網路工具分享資訊，例如：臉書、推特、電話軟體和那類的東西。

美化句子	I share information with friends via various online tools, **such as** Facebook, Twitter, **and other** social media. 我透過各種線上工具與朋友分享訊息，像是：臉書、推特和其他的社交媒體。

舉一反三 1	Various beverages are available on the plane, **such as** juice, water, **and other** soft drinks. 各式飲料都可在飛機上取用，包括：果汁、水和其他軟性飲料。

舉一反三 2	People appreciate impressive architecture in the world, **such as** Taipei 101 Building, Dubai City Tower, **and other** famous skyscrapers. 人們很欣賞世上令人讚嘆的建築物，例如：台北 101 大樓、杜拜塔和其他有名的摩天大樓。

自由發揮	

＊可參考訊號字類別 ⑭

套用句型 70 For one thing S + V... And for another S + V...

初級句子	I like to work in small companies, because colleagues are friendly, and because they can change more quickly. 我喜歡在小公司上班，因為同事較友善，也因為小公司改變較快。

美化句子	I like to work in small companies. **For one thing**, they are more personal. **And for another**, they can react to market changes more quickly. 我喜歡在小公司上班。一方面是較有人情味，另一方面是對市場變化反應較快。

舉一反三 1	I like to live in big cities. **For one thing**, they have convenient subway systems. **And for another**, there are more recreational places in big cities. 我喜歡住在大都市。一方面是因為有方便的地鐵系統，另一方面是有較多的娛樂活動。
舉一反三 2	I enjoy watching dance performances. **For one thing**, dancing is very beautiful. **And for another**, it helps me to reflect on the meaning of life. 我喜歡看舞蹈表演。一方面是因為舞蹈很優美，另一方面是它反映了生活的意義。
自由發揮 🖉	

＊可參考訊號字類別 ⑭

套用句型 71 [something] indicates an imminent [something].

| 初級句子 | The company's sales revenue is getting worse, so it is in danger.
公司業績變得更差，所以公司有危險。 |

| 美化句子 | The plunging sales revenue **indicates an imminent** crisis.
持續下滑的業績意味著公司即將面臨危機。 |

| 舉一反三 1 | The gathering clouds and strong wind **indicate an imminent** typhoon.
密佈的烏雲和強風顯示強烈颱風快來了。 |

| 舉一反三 2 | Little differentiation between the two products **indicates an imminent** price war.
兩商品的差異化很小意味著接下來會有價格戰了。 |

| 自由發揮✎ | |

[someone] is / are reluctant to [do something].

初級句子	I don't want to do the job. 我不想做那工作。

⇩

美化句子	I **am reluctant to** take on the responsibility. 我不是很願意承擔那責任。

舉一反三 1	Mr. Jones **is reluctant to** accept the proposals. 瓊斯先生不是很願意接受那些提議。

舉一反三 2	We **are reluctant to** sell the house. 我們不是很想賣掉房子。

自由發揮 ✐	

套用句型 73 **When I [did something] for the first time, I felt extremely [adj.]**

初級句子	When I made my first presentation, I felt very nervous. 當我第一次做簡報時，我感到非常緊張。

美化句子	**When I** presented a science project in front of the class **for the first time, I felt extremely** nervous. 當我第一次在課堂上做科學簡報，我感到異常地緊張。

舉一反三 1	**When I** arranged a formal business meeting **for the first time, I felt extremely** tense. 當我第一次安排正式的商務會議，我感到相當地緊張。

舉一反三 2	**When I** won the Best-Sales-Rep award **for the first time, I felt extremely** inspired. 當我第一次贏得最佳業務的獎項，我感到極度地鼓舞。

自由發揮	

套用句型 ⑦ Although [S. + V.]..., [S. + V.]...

初級句子	We Taiwanese students learn English, but our teachers only teach grammar not speaking skills. 我們台灣學生學英文，但老師只教文法，而非口說技巧。

美化句子	**Although** students in Taiwan take English courses, Taiwanese teachers focus too much on teaching grammar rules rather than speaking fluency. 雖說在台灣學生也上英文課，台灣老師將焦點放在教文法上，而非口語流利。

舉一反三 1	**Although** organizations prepare business plans, the majority of managers focus too much on executing details rather than understanding industry trends. 雖說公司都有準備業務計劃，多數經理人將焦點放在執行細節上，而非瞭解產業趨勢。

舉一反三 2	**Although** global decisions have been made to reduce the problems of pollution and climate change, the solutions have not yet taken effect. 雖說全球都決定要解決環境污染與氣候變遷的問題，解決方案尚未見效。

自由發揮 ✐	

＊可參考訊號字類別 ⑨

套用句型 75 **Part of the problem might be that [someone] have an incomplete understanding of how + Adj. + [something] is.**

初級句子

Directors don't know if the market is mature or not, and that's the problem.

總理不瞭解市場是否成熟，那是個問題。

美化句子

Part of the problem might be that directors have an incomplete understanding of how mature the market is.

一部份的問題在於總理對市場是否成熟沒有全面性的瞭解。

舉一反三 1

Part of the problem might be that parents have an incomplete understanding of how developed the infant brain is.

一部份的問題在於父母對嬰兒腦力是如何發展的缺乏全面性的瞭解。

舉一反三 2

Part of the problem might be that stakeholders have an incomplete understanding of how effective the strategy is.

一部份的問題在於關係人對策略是否有效並沒有全面性的瞭解。

自由發揮 ✎

One disadvantage of [something] is that + S. + V....

初級句子

Using smart-phones is not good because they waste our time.
使用智慧型手機不好，因為會浪費時間。

美化句子

One disadvantage of smart-phones **is that** they potentially decrease worker productivity.
智慧型手機的一個缺點是，有可能降低員工的生產力。

舉一反三 1

One disadvantage of drinking alcohol **is that** it's harmful to the health.
飲酒的一個壞處是，酒精對人體健康有害。

舉一反三 2

One disadvantage of nuclear energy **is that** it's not a renewable source of energy.
核能的一個缺點是，其並非一種可再生利用的能源。

自由發揮 🖉

＊可參考訊號字類別 ⑮

套用句型 77 [something] be not suitable in [today's situation].

初級句子

We use old sales methods, but those are not suitable anymore.
我們使用舊的銷售方式，但那些不再適用了。

美化句子

Traditional sales methods **are not suitable in** today's competitive market.
傳統的銷售方式不適合在現在競爭激烈的市場上使用。

舉一反三 1

Some out-dated learning strategies **are not suitable in** today's educational environment.
一些過時的學習策略不適合在現今的教育環境使用。

舉一反三 2

Old-school English vocabulary **is not suitable in** today's dynamic workplace.
老派的英文單字不適合在今日多變的工作場合使用。

自由發揮 ✏️

套用句型 78 All these explanations make it clear that + S. + V....

初級句子	After explaining, we can see that everybody should save natural resources together. 經過解釋後，我們可以看到每個人都應該共同保育天然資源。

美化句子	**All these explanations make it clear that** it is everyone's responsibility to save natural resources. 一切的解釋讓我們更加明白，保育天然資源是每個人的責任。

舉一反三 1	**All these explanations make it clear that** all team members should collaborate in order to achieve the goal. 一切的解釋讓我們更加明白，所有同仁應密切合作以達成目標。

舉一反三 2	**All these explanations make it clear that** persistence is indispensable for career success. 一切的解釋讓我們更加明白，堅持下去是職涯成功的不二法門。

自由發揮 ✎	

套用句型 79 It can be seen that + S. + V....

初級句子	It proves what I say: the world around us keeps changing. 這就證明了我說的：我們的世界不停地在變化。

美化句子	**It can be seen that** the world around us is constantly evolving. 很明顯地，我們的世界持續演化。

舉一反三 1	**It can be seen that** people should manage time more wisely. 很顯然地，人們應該更有效地善用時間。

舉一反三 2	**It can be seen that** distractions hamper worker productivity. 由此可見，讓人分心的瑣事會阻礙員工的生產力。

自由發揮 ✎	

＊可參考訊號字類別 ⑯

套用句型 ⑧⓪ To put it simply, S. + V....

初級句子	It's a simple idea to understand that people shouldn't work overtime. 這簡單的概念很容易瞭解，人們不應該加班。

美化句子	**To put it simply**, overtime should be avoided if there is no particular need. 簡單來說，若沒特殊需要的話，就儘量避免加班。

舉一反三 1	**To put it simply**, continuous improvement is the best hedge against future risk. 簡單來說，持續地進步是對抗未知風險最佳的保障。

舉一反三 2	**To put it simply**, a good leader should establish and maintain credibility. 簡單來說，一位好的經理人應該建立並保持自身的信用。

自由發揮✐	

＊可參考訊號字類別 ⑯

Chapter 2

正式寫作

UNIT 3　掌握寫作架構

　　英文 essay 類的文章會給一個具論述價值的題目，要求考生表達看法，並舉出實際例子當例證來加以解釋原因。因此，一篇完整的 essay 文章內自然要包括：看法 (topic sentence) 與例證 (specific example) 兩大元素。再加上開場 (opening) 段落與結論 (conclusion) 段落，整體的結構便如右頁表格呈現。

一、掌握論述文 Essay 寫作策略

❶ 徹底瞭解題目

　　一般考生最常犯的錯誤之一是文章內容「文不對題」。在沒有充份地瞭解題目所問的要點之下，就貿然下筆，導致最後內容偏掉了，沒有精準地針對問題來回答。

　　比方說，題目問的是 Do you prefer to work in the office or work from home?「你喜歡在公司工作還是在家工作？」，那麼同學應該就此問題「二選一」，由 work in the office 或 work from home 兩者當中選一個自己的偏好來討論，並舉實例以說明確切的原因。

　　但是若同學寫成這樣 "Why do people work? Some people might think that we work because we have to make a living. But for me, it's not about the money actually. I work because I find what I do meaningful and I can make a difference to the world." 「人們為何要工作？有些人認為我們工作是為了生活。但對我來說，這不光是錢的問題。我工作是因為我覺得我的工作很有意義，並可以讓世界不同。」以上變成在討論「工作的意義」了。答題沒有針對題目所問的「在公司上班 vs. 在家上班」兩者擇一討論的話，就會被視為離題。

沒有針對題目作答的離題內容，不管字彙或文法使用得再優美，都還是會被視爲嚴重的錯誤。因此，看到題目時同學不要很心急地想趕緊寫內容，務必先仔細地考慮題目所要問的眞正要點，並針對所問的要點規劃出結構 (organization)。

② 總架構 (Organization)

　　註：上述所提及的 Developmental paragraphs 三個意見發展的段落，為建議／參考寫法。若因有些考試的規定時間較短，字數限制也較少，那麼便不一定要發展到三個段落，僅發展「兩個意見」段落也無妨喔！本書內以下所有例子亦同。

EXERCISE 1

請針對以下這些題目，點出關鍵點和規劃所需討論的正確方向：

Q1 **What are top 3 qualities of a good supervisor?**

討論要點

Q2 **Should schools require students to wear uniforms?**

討論要點

Q3 **How to develop children's sense of responsibility?**

討論要點

Q4 **Should government focus on improving the Internet or public transportation systems?**

討論要點

本書附錄中，另外還收錄了 238 個經常考的寫作題目，提供讀者進行更多樣的寫作練習。

EXERCISE 1 · 例解

Q1. What are top 3 qualities of a good supervisor?

討論
要點

Idea#1 –
Excellent communication skills – A good supervisor should be able to communicate clearly and correctly.

Idea#2 –
Welcome challenges – An efficient supervisor should be well prepared to challenges and adapt to new changes.

Idea#3 –
Strategic thinking ability – A capable supervisor should understand market trends, customers' demands and even competitors' next moves.

Q2. Should schools require students to wear uniforms?

討論
要點

Idea#1 –
Wearing uniforms increases students' self-confidence.

Idea#2 –
School uniforms ensures student safety on campus.

Idea#3 –
Uniforms could also lessen distractions in the classroom.

Q3. How to develop children's sense of responsibility?

討論
要點

Idea#1 –

Ask children to actively get involved in family projects.

Idea#2 –

Give children clear and positive instructions for doing tasks and compliment them when they are done.

Idea#3 –

Parents should be a good role model, as children always imitate what they see parents do.

Q4. Should government focus on improving the Internet or public transportation systems?

討論
要點

Opinion –

The government should balance budget and resources equally between these two developments.

Idea#1 –

Implementing the Internet to respond to the increasing demands of an information society.

Idea#2 –

A well-organized public transportation system in inevitable for a country's prosperity.

❸ 組織想法

　　徹底地瞭解題目所問的要點之後，腦中應立即浮現一組「架構框框」，並思考針對此題目的 topic sentence 為何，與有什麼實例可以舉出應用的。比方說，針對同一題目 "Do you prefer to work in the office or work from home?" 來構思，架構框框內的初稿要點可能會是：

Topic Do you prefer to work in the office or work from home?			
Thesis statement: I hold that **working in the office** is better.			表態以選擇討論「在公司工作」較好。
Idea#1	Topic sentence	Working in the office makes workers be able to **focus entirely on their tasks**.	說明「在公司工作」的第一個好處是，可以專心在任務上。
	Specific example	Ms. Marissa Mayer of Yahoo requires all her employees to work in the office in order to maintain speed and quality of work.	使用 Yahoo 公司 Ms. Mayer 的意見當實例。
Idea#2	Topic sentence	Workers can get **involved in discussions more easily** in the office.	說明「在公司工作」的第二個優點是，可以跟同事面對面討論。
	Specific example	I myself participate in meetings and exchange creative ideas with colleagues in the office.	使用自己參與會議的經驗當例子。
Idea#3	Topic sentence	People working from home might be **distracted by interruptions** from children or neighbors.	第三要點通常可以活用變化一下，討論反方，也就是「在家工作」可能會有的缺點。
	Specific example	My two children require my attention all the time. It's hard for me to fully concentrate on my work.	使用家中小孩會使工作分心的例子。

由此可以看出，針對一個題目若可以先將架構規劃好，適切地擺入意見「主題句」與先想好可運作的「實際例子」的話，隨後在發展全文上，將會簡易許多。因此，建議同學平時在練習準備時，可以善加利用以下表格，依不同題目的要點，將點子意見的架構先規劃出來喔！

EXERCISE 2

請針對以下題目規劃出文章架構：

Topic 1 Should teachers receive advanced training regularly?

Thesis statement:

Idea#1	Topic sentence	
	Specific example	

Idea#2	Topic sentence	
	Specific example	

Idea#3	Topic sentence	
	Specific example	

Topic 2 Do you prefer to work for a large enterprise or a small company?

Thesis statement:

| Idea#1 | Topic sentence | |
| | Specific example | |

| Idea#2 | Topic sentence | |
| | Specific example | |

| Idea#3 | Topic sentence | |
| | Specific example | |

 **EXERCISE 2** • 例解

Topic 1 Should teachers receive advanced training regularly?

Thesis statement:
Teachers should take advanced training regularly to sharpen their knowledge and skills.

Idea#1	Topic sentence	Teachers acquiring the latest and firsthand knowledge are able to maintain their competitive advantages and irreplaceability.
	Specific example	I was especially impressed by an exceptional teacher in the university who <u>returned to the US at least once every two years to capture the latest business and management concepts</u>.
Idea#2	Topic sentence	Receiving advanced training qualifies teachers to provide students with up-to-date information.
	Specific example	Ten years ago, one of my teachers spent extra time taking iPad training classes, thus he was able to take advantage of the mobility of an iPad and present course-related data or photos on the Internet. This approach deepened students' impressions on the lecture and stimulated students' interests in learning.
Idea#3	Topic sentence	Some teachers might consider that since they are granted tenure already and it is pointless for them to acquire updated knowledge consistently.
	Specific example	This idea is inapplicable to today's competitive society. If a teacher is reluctant to sharpen his skills to keep up with the world, he is not likely to guide his students toward the appropriate directions.

Thesis statement:

I think working for a large corporation has certain advantages over working for a small business.

Idea#1	Topic sentence	Large corporations often provide extra job benefits and perks that small companies can't afford to offer.
	Specific example	My husband used to work at IBM and the company provided on-line gyms, child care and other additional benefits for employees.
Idea#2	Topic sentence	The stability of a job is an obvious advantage of working for a large enterprise.
	Specific example	One of my friends works at Microsoft Taiwan Corp. and he rarely worries on a regular basis about whether the company will fold.
Idea#3	Topic sentence	Large companies provide employees with state-of-the-art facilities to use in the office.
	Specific example	Employees at Microsoft Taiwan don't worry about the availability of high-tech devices, such as photocopiers or high-speed Internet connection, and thus can concentrate entirely on their tasks.

❹ 做好時間的分配

　　各種類型的考試在英文 essay 寫作部份的時間規定稍有不同，有 20 分鐘內需完成 150 字的，40 分鐘內完成 250 字，或 30 分鐘內完成 350 字的規定。但不管是哪種時間限制，考生自己都應做好時間的規劃，比方說，30 分鐘內花 3 分鐘構思，25 分鐘書寫，2 分鐘檢查等。最好是可以完成「全文有頭有尾」的狀態，而非一開始花過多時間，導致寫不完沒有結論段，如此會被視為 incomplete 的文章，分數自然不會高。

　　此外，一篇文章有了明確的意見，和實際的例子當佐證，固然是一篇結構完整的文章了。但是，若文章內的句子錯誤百出，錯別字過多，文法句型也使用得不恰當，甚至於明明不瞭解的慣用語也亂用的話，不但會讓閱卷者難以瞭解意思，還會被視為嚴重的錯誤。因此，基本文法概念、文法句型、遣詞用字等，需仔細斟酌使用，並隨時檢查文法細節或單字拼法是否正確。若非自己非常熟悉並確定用法正確的句型或單字，便不要貿然使用。

　　接下來的各章節中，我們將分別針對一篇文章應有架構的四個大項目 (Opening / Topic sentence / Specific example / Conclusion) 來做更細節的討論。

二、開場段落 (Opening)

　　很多同學寫 essay 類文章時，劈頭就以「I think...」（我認為……）來啟始說明自己的看法。但如此開頭方式很可能讓讀者（針對考試來說，也就是閱卷的考官）摸不著頭緒，在尚未完全瞭解討論什麼主題的情況下，也很難判斷看法是否有道理。因此，為了要讓讀者／考官有效地瞭解作者對某事件的觀點，文章的開頭部份應先「引題」，先就議題本身做些簡短的說明，讀者／考官才知道是在討論什麼主題。

　　一般來說，開場白段落的內容需要包括以下三大部份：

第一句：解釋背景 (General background)
第二句：帶入題目 (Introducing the argument)
第三句：意見表態 (Thesis statement)

① 📄 **開場段落第一句怎麼寫？**

A. 解釋議題的背景

首先，開場段落的第一句功能是，可針對要討論的議題之背景稍作介紹。

比方說，要討論的題目是：

題目	Why students choose to study abroad? （學生為什麼選擇出國留學？）

那麼針對此題目的切入便可以是：

開場 第一句	**Nowadays university graduates can choose freely where to pursue further education.** （現今大學畢業生可以自由地選擇在哪裡取得更高的教育。）

又比方說，若題目討論的是：

題目	What are some advantages of the Internet? （網路的好處有哪些？）

那麼啟始句便可針對「the Internet」的概念切入：

開場 第一句	**No one can deny the significance of the Internet. The Internet has made this world a global village.** （沒人可以否認網路的重要性。網路儼然讓世界轉變成為一個地球村了。）

B. 使用個人經驗

若初學的同學造句能力尚未很純熟，想利用更精簡的方式開頭，也可以使用「個人經驗」來起始。此方式的好處是，既然是使用個人經驗，便不用強記任何資訊，寫起來較可得心應手。比方說，若題目問：

題目	Do you think that the government should build more parking towers in the city? （你認為政府是否應在市區內蓋更多停車塔？）

那麼利用個人經驗起始的句子便可以是：

開場 第一句	**Whenever I drive to the city, I always have difficulty finding somewhere to park.** （每當我開車進城，我總是找不到停車位。）

再來一個例子，若問題是：

題目	Do you think high school students should be required to wear uniforms? （你認為高中生應該穿制服嗎？）

便可使用個人經驗帶出首句：

開場 第一句	**I happened to read an article in the May issue of Education Magazine discussing the pros and cons of requiring students to wear uniforms.** （我剛好在五月份的「教育雜誌」上看到一篇討論要求學生穿制服之利弊的文章。）

C. 直接切入主題

還有一種情況是，寫作時間很短（可能僅二十分鐘），且字數也限制在 150 字以內，可能沒有過多時間描述題目背景或帶入個人經驗，那麼這種情況可使用「直接切入主題」的方式開頭。

比方說，題目問：

題目	Which city in Taiwan would you recommend your foreign friends to visit? （你會推薦外國朋友參觀台灣的哪個都市？）

透過直接切入主題的方式寫的起始句會是：

開場 第一句	**If I needed to suggest just one city for my foreign friends to visit, it would definitely have to be Taipei.** （若我要推薦一個都市給外國朋友，那我一定會請他們來台北市旅遊。）

再提一個例子，若題目問的是：

題目	Do you think the government should focus on building the Internet or public transportation systems? （你認爲政府應該將焦點放在建網路還是建大眾運輸系統上？）

那麼若使用直接切入主題的方式開頭，起始句子可以是：

開場 第一句	**The issue to be considered here is whether the government should focus more on building the Internet or public transportation systems.** （此處要討論的議題是，政府應該將焦點放在建網路還是建大眾運輸系統上。）

　　綜合以上，考生寫 essay 題時通常會有的「我第一句要寫什麼？」的困擾，可以使用上述三種方式擇一來解決，包括：**解釋背景、個人經驗和直接切入題目**。考生可依各式考試不同的時間與字述限制等要求，選擇一種恰當的開頭方式。

❷ 📄 開場段落第二句怎麼寫？

　　開場段落的首句將背景稍加解釋之後，接著第二句的作用便是「引題」，要將題目介紹出來了。此時可以使用以下幾種句型來引題：

- ✓ **This leads me to wonder whether** + 題目
- ✓ **This raises the question of whether** + 題目
- ✓ **This results in different views on whether** + 題目
- ✓ **Different views thus exist about whether** + 題目

比方說，題目為：

題目	Should people pursue a challenging goal/dream or a more practical one? （人們應該追求具挑戰性的目標／夢想還是較實際一點的目標呢？）

那麼，首句背景解釋句可以是：

開場 第一句	**No matter how big or small our dreams are, they have significant importance in our lives.** （不管我們的夢想是大是小，他們對我們生命來說都相當重要。）

接著，第二句引題便會是：

第二句 引題	**This results in different views on whether people should pursue a challenging or a more practical goal.** （這便引起不同的看法了：人們應該追求挑戰性的還是較實際的目標呢？）

❸ 📄 開場段落第三句怎麼寫？

引入題目之後，開場段落的最後一句便是「表態句」了，也就是最重要的「thesis statement」。此句的目的不僅是明確地表達出自己的立場，還是全文可以發展下去的骨幹。也就是說，接下來的三個（或兩個）developmental paragraphs 意見段落，都要根據在 thesis statement 內所設定的立場來發展。表態句的呈現方式，可以使用以下幾種句型：

- ✓ **My view is that** + 表態

☑ **I would say that** ＋ 表態

☑ **I hold the belief that** ＋ 表態

☑ **I take the position that** ＋ 表態

再度拿上一個例子來討論：

題目	Should people pursue a challenging goal/dream or a more practical one? （人們應該追求具挑戰性的目標／夢想還是較實際一點的目標呢？）

開場 第一句	**No matter how big or small our dreams are, they have significant importance in our lives.** （不管我們的夢想是大是小，他們對我們生命來說都相當重要。）

第二句 引題	**This results in different views on whether people should pursue a challenging or a more practical goal.** （這便引起不同的看法了：人們應該追求挑戰性的還是較實際的目標呢？）

接下來表態句可以是：

第三句 表態	**I am of the view that people should focus their efforts fully on a more workable goal.** （我的看法是人們應該將精力專注在完成可行的目標上。）

　　上述的表態句非常明確，就是在 a challenging goal 和 a practical goal 兩者間選擇其一，要討論的是 a practical goal 了。此處，同學應該可以發覺，**表態句將題目選項帶入的同時，還要經過「換字」的處理。最好不是直接將題目逐字抄下，而是應該經過理解後，換個方式用自己的話表達改寫**，以此題的例子來看便是「practical」換字為「workable」。

❹ 📄 五個開場段落寫作範例

　　接下來，我們便把上述討論的 essay 文章開場段落書寫方式，加上實際的題目，

168

整理出以下 5 個範例給同學參考：

範例 **1**

Question Do you agree or disagree with the following statement? The ability to read and write is more important now than in the past.

Opening:

This issue to be considered here is whether the ability to read and write is more important now than in the past. While some people might think that such literacy ability is vital regardless of which time period. I still hold the belief that reading and writing ability is far more necessary in this competitive world than in the past.

題目　你同不同意以下觀點？讀和寫的能力在現在來說比過去更重要。

開場段落　此議題要討論的是，讀與寫的能力在現今來說是否比以往更重要。有些人可能會認為，這讀寫能力不管在任何時期都是很重要的。我還是會認為，讀寫能力在今日競爭如此激烈的市場上遠比在過去更加需要！

範例 **2**

Question Do you think people should take risks or experience new things when they are young or when they are older?

Opening:

When considering whether people should take as many risks as possible and experience challenges when they are still young or after they getting older, opinions from people with different backgrounds may vary. I personally hold the belief that people ought to pursue challenges when they are still young and embrace more experiences, the better.

題目　你認為人們應該在年輕時就去冒險或體驗新事物，還是等老了再做？

開場段落　當討論到人們是否應該趁年輕時就儘量冒險和體驗挑戰事物，還是要等老一點再體驗，不同背景的人之意見自然也會不同。我個人是認為，人們應該趁年輕時就迎向挑戰，並且擁抱多點經驗會更好。

範例 3

Question Do you agree or disagree with the following statement? In order to become well-informed, one has to get information from different news resources.

Opening:

Every minute of every day, something newsworthy is happening somewhere in the world. This leads me to wonder whether people need to acquire information from various news resources in order to keep well-informed. I believe that people should obtain reliable facts from different news resources.

題目　你同不同意以下觀點？爲了得知周遭所發生的事，人們應自多種新聞來源取得資訊。

開場段落　每天的每分每秒，在世界的各個角落都可能會有新聞發生。這就讓我思索，人們是否應該要自不同的新聞來源取得資訊以得知天下事呢？我相信人們應該自各式新聞來源取得可靠的資訊。

範例 4

Question Which city in Taiwan would you recommend your foreign friends to visit?

Opening:

If I needed to suggest just one city for my foreign friends to visit, it would definitely have to be Taipei. Not only is Taipei the place in which I was born, but it also is an international city worth visiting in Taiwan.

題目　你會建議外國朋友到台灣的哪個都市旅遊呢？

開場段落　若我需要推薦外國朋友值得一遊的都市，那就一定會是台北了。不僅僅是因爲台北是我生長的地方，她同時也是在台灣的值得一遊的國際化都市。

Question Do you prefer to live in a big city or in a small town?

Opening:

Some people opt to live in big cities, while others like the natural and quiet surrounding in the countryside. As far as I am concerned, I would like to live in a big city for sure. I think living in a big city enables me to widen my perspectives than living in a small town.

題目　你喜歡住在大都市還是小村莊？

開場段落　有些人會選擇住在大都市，有些人則喜歡自然和安靜的鄉村環境。就我來看，我當然是喜歡住在大都市。我認爲住在大都市比住在小村莊更可以讓我拓展視野。

三、文章主體-1：主題句 (Topic Sentence)

❶ 如何構思主題句？

在寫完開場段落之後，接著就是文章的主體部份的撰寫了。文章主體至少要包含兩個發展段落 (Developmental Paragraphs)。每一個發展段落都要有一句「主題句」(Topic Sentence)。主題句的作用是針對在開場段落所寫的 thesis statement 列出原因並控制發展段落所要發展的方向。

書寫主題句時，可以參考下列幾個要點：

A 先在腦中構思好，題目的焦點爲何，要確實地針對題目焦點回答，並發想什麼點子是比較合理又好發揮的。比方說，若題目是問 Do you prefer to work at home or work in the office?（你喜歡在家工作還是在辦公室工作？）那麼假設您決定要討論 work in the office 的好處，在腦中就應馬上構思出至少兩個在辦公室工作的優點，可能是「較可專心，工作效率較高」與「方便與同事討論交換意見」等。

B 接著將此兩個點子寫成句子，比方說上述的例子，成形的英文主題句會是：

- Working in the office enables employees to focus entirely on their tasks.
  （在辦公室上班讓員工可以專心執行任務。）

- Working in the office makes coworkers get involved in discussion more easily.
（在辦公室上班讓同事間可以隨時討論。）

C 若是列出主題句當中，發現某個點子跟題目焦點關係不大，或無法真正支持到 thesis statement，那麼就應該將偏題的點子捨棄。比方說在 work at home vs. work in the office 題目當中，若主題句寫 I always commute to my office by subways.（我通常是搭地鐵去辦公室。）這樣的句子和 thesis statement 所提的「在辦公室工作的優點」並無關連性，便不應出現在主題句中。

D 另外，有些英檢考試寫作時間較長（30~40 分鐘），要求的是五段式作文，字數也較多。在此已有兩個要點的情況下，若要發展第三個要點，可以有兩個選擇。其一是再提第三個在辦公室工作的好處，其二是可以發揮一下批判思考的能力，討論一下反方的「在家工作」可能會有的缺點，以藉此說明是什麼樣的理由，讓您不選擇在家工作呢？那麼根據一樣的題目，第三個討論反方的主題句，便可能會是：

- People working from home might find various distractions challenging to their productivity.
（在家工作的人可能會發現各種讓人分心的事物會降低他們的生產力。）

E 如此三個主題句就成形了。最後，為了讓點子之間順暢地聯貫起來，我們可以使用適當的 transitional expressions，類似像 To begin with、Furthermore、In contrast 等用語。若使用這些用語將三個主題句串起來，就會如下列所示：

Question	Do you prefer to work at home or work in the office?
Thesis statement	I hold the belief that **working in the office** is more beneficial than working at home.
Topic sentence #1	**First of all**, working in the office enables employees to focus entirely on their tasks.
Topic sentence #2	**Secondly**, working in the office makes coworkers get involved in discussion more easily.
Topic sentence #3	**In contrast**, people working from home might find various distractions challenging to their productivity.

接著，請再參考下列五組發展主題句的範例。

❷ 🔖 **五個發展主題句範例**

範例 1

Question What are some ways people use to reduce stress?

Thesis statement:

In my opinion, some effective ways of reducing stress are exercise, reading books and listening to music.

Topic sentence #1	**To begin with**, being active can increase people's sense of well-being and distract them from daily worries.
Topic sentence #2	**Next**, reading can be a brilliant and healthy escape from the stress of everyday life.
Topic sentence #3	**Finally**, listening to music is a relatively effective and inexpensive way to quickly sooth people's mind.

中譯

問題	人們會用什麼方式來減輕壓力？
論點	在我看來，可以用來減輕壓力的有效方式包括：運動，看書，和聽音樂。
主題句 #1	首先，活動起來可以增加人們的幸福感，也可讓人從日常擔憂的事中脫離。
主題句 #2	再者，看書是個不錯且健康的方式，讓人可以由每日的生活壓力中抽離。
主題句 #3	最後，聽音樂是相對有效又不花錢的方式，可以很快地讓人心情平靜下來。

Question Do you agree or disagree with the statement? People's external appearance is more important than anything else.

Thesis statement:

I disagree with the title statement. Instead, I think that a person's inner quality and virtue are more important qualities to consider.

Topic sentence #1	**First of all**, it is the real inner quality of a person that goes far beyond just external appearance.
Topic sentence #2	**Furthermore**, what people really concern would be a person's capability and performance.
Topic sentence #3	**On the contrary**, uncritical evaluation on a person's appearance may lead us to a mistake in judgement.

中譯

問題	你同不同意此論述?人們的外表比任何事物都重要。
論點	我不同意此論點。相反地,我認為一個人的內在特質與優點才是考量的重點。
主題句 #1	首先,一個人的內在才是讓人超越外在容貌的真正特質。
主題句 #2	更甚者,人們真正關心的是一個人是否有能力和表現。
主題句 #3	反之,若對一個人的外表做出不當的評估可能會導致我們做出錯誤的判斷。

Question Is hard-working the only key toward career success?

Thesis statement:

I deem that hard-working is just an ingredient of success, not the only key.

Topic sentence #1	**First**, in order to bring about success, hard-work has to be directed by clear and practical goals.
Topic sentence #2	**Additionally**, intelligence and imagination play vital roles toward success as well.
Topic sentence #3	**Last but not least**, persistence is equally essential to success.

中譯

問題　　努力工作是職涯成功的唯一要素嗎？

論點　　我認為努力工作只是通往成功道路上的一個環節，不是唯一的要素。

主題句 #1　首先，要達到成功，努力的方面也需要靠明確又實際的目標來指引。

主題句 #2　另外，智慧與想像力對成功與否也發揮重要的角色。

主題句 #3　最後，要有毅力與成功同等重要。

Question Do you agree with this statement? Advertising is a waste of time and money because customers already know what they want.

Thesis statement:

I consider that the real value and effectiveness of advertising really depend on what industry and product type we are talking about.

Topic sentence #1	**To begin with**, advertising does play a critical role in promoting commodities or services, since it's one of the most direct ways to communicate with target audience.
Topic sentence #2	**However**, the effectiveness of advertising might be less apparent in specific industries.

中譯

問題	你是否同意此觀點？廣告是浪費時間又浪費錢，因爲客戶早已知道他們要什麼。
論點	我認爲廣告的眞正價値與效果，是要看何種產業和產品型式而定。
主題句 #1	首先，在推廣一般日常產品或服務時，廣告的確扮演著重要角色，因此廣告是最直接可以跟目標客群溝通的方式之一。
主題句 #2	然而，對一些特定的產業來說廣告的效用可能就不那麼明顯了。

Question Do you think all school teachers should be required to take courses regularly to update their knowledge?

Thesis statement:

From my point of view, teachers should take advanced trainings periodically in order to sharpen their knowledge and skills.

Topic sentence #1	**First of all**, teachers acquiring the latest and firsthand knowledge are able to maintain their competitive advantages and irreplaceability.
Topic sentence #2	**Moreover**, receiving advanced training qualifies teachers to provide student with up-to-date information.
Topic sentence #3	**In contrast**, teachers who are reluctant to sharpen their skills might not be able to guide their students toward appropriate directions.

中譯

問題	你認為學校老師都應該要定期上課接收新知嗎？
論點	在我看來，老師應該定期接受進階訓練，以增進他們的知識和技能。
主題句 #1	首先，有吸收新的第一手資料的老師，可以維持他們的競爭優勢和不可取代性。
主題句 #2	再者，接受新的第一手資訊的老師可以提供學生最新的資訊。
主題句 #3	相反地，不願意精進技能的老師，可能就無法領導學生走向恰當的方向。

EXERCISE 寫作練習

請利用本章開場段落 (unit 3-2) 的 **5** 個範例，延伸寫出「主題句」：
【在學習後面兩個章節之後，再補上細節例證與結論】

- Unit 3-4（文章主體 -2：細節例證）後的寫作練習 (P189)，請在此處填上五篇文章的 Specific example。
- Unit 3-5（結論段落）後的寫作練習 (P197)，請在此處填上五篇文章的 Conclusion。

①

Question Do you agree or disagree with the following statement? The ability to read and write is more important now than in the past.

Opening:

This issue to be considered here is whether the ability to read and write is more important now than in the past. While some people might think that such literacy ability is vital regardless of which time period. I still hold the belief that reading and writing ability is far more necessary in this competitive world than in the past.

Topic sentence #1	
Specific example	

Topic sentence #2	
Specific example	
Topic sentence #3	
Specific example	
Conclusion	

②

Question Do you think people should take risks or experience new things when they are young or when they are older?

Opening:

When considering whether people should take as many risks as possible and experience challenges when they are still young or after they getting older, opinions from people with different backgrounds may vary. I personally hold the belief that people ought to pursue challenges when they are still young and embrace more experiences, the better.

Topic sentence #1	
Specific example	
Topic sentence #2	
Specific example	
Topic sentence #3	
Specific example	
Conclusion	

③

Question Do you agree or disagree with the following statement? In order to become well-informed, one has to get information from different news resources.

Opening:

Every minute of every day, something newsworthy is happening somewhere in the world. This leads me to wonder whether people need to acquire information from various news resources in order to keep well-informed. I believe that people should obtain reliable facts from different news resources.

Topic sentence #1	
Specific example	
Topic sentence #2	
Specific example	
Topic sentence #3	
Specific example	
Conclusion	

④

Question Which city in Taiwan would you recommend your foreign friends to visit?

Opening:	
If I needed to suggest just one city for my foreign friends to visit, it would definitely have to be Taipei. Not only is Taipei the place in which I was born, but it also is an international city worth visiting in Taiwan.	
Topic sentence #1	
Specific example	
Topic sentence #2	
Specific example	
Topic sentence #3	
Specific example	
Conclusion	

⑤

Question Do you prefer to live in a big city or in a small town?

Opening:

Some people opt to live in big cities, while others like the natural and quiet surrounding in the countryside. As far as I am concerned, I would like to live in a big city for sure. I think living in a big city enables me to widen my perspectives than living in a small town.

Topic sentence #1	
Specific example	
Topic sentence #2	
Specific example	
Topic sentence #3	
Specific example	
Conclusion	

四、文章主體-2：細節例證 (Supporting Facts)

如同先前提到過的，每個人背景，想法，意見本來就都不相同，針對某一議題的闡述更是沒有所謂的「標準答案」。自己認為如何都無妨，有任何天馬行空的點子都可以，重要的是要有「實例」來當證據，以便更可以說服他人。在考試時，要寫會得高分的文章，不可能是靠背「模板」，和四處抓來的用語試圖拼拼湊湊、疊床架屋就可以過關的。文章結構完整，用字也還算精準固然可以掙得一些分數。但若文章空有其表，內容卻了無新意，看不出作者要表達的點子和別人的有何特出之處，讓人過目即忘，還是無法將分數差距拉大的。

① 四大類細節例證

因此，要寫出「與他人有所不同，不重覆」的內容，可以在「舉實例」部份做出區隔。要舉出具說服力的事證、實例，可以靠在日常生活當中的積累與觀察。比方說：

◇ **個人的經驗**：既然是自身的經驗，親身經歷過，而非背頌模板內容的，自然最好發揮了。建議同學多使用跟自身經驗相關的實例。

◇ **對他人的觀察所歸納出之看法**：即便不是自己親身經歷過的事，我們也可以由周遭親朋好友，老師或同學等處得到資訊。這些由別人經驗的分享的真實事例，也適合當實例。

◇ **現實生活中的現況**：我們生活的周遭充滿了可以應用的材料。可能是台北的捷運，夜市的小吃，或各種文化活動等，運用起來都可以讓文章更添生動。

◇ **名人成功經驗**：要寫具說服力的內容，使用名人的事蹟是最好不過的了。比方說 Bill Gates、Steve Jobs 或 Mark Zuckerberg 的成功經驗或他們說過的智慧之語等，都可以讓讀者感同身受。

另外，若自己在某權威報章雜誌或論文看到特殊的見解，聽到某場與眾不同的演講，或在社群網路上看到他人的分享等，也都是適合當寫作材料的內容。以下我們便由五種不同的角度來看舉實例的運用。

範例 1 以「社會現況」來當實例

Question Advantages of the Internet

Topic sentence:

The Internet is such a modern and prevalent tool that people depend heavily on for daily communication.

Example:

For example, in Taipei our government has implemented the wireless network in response to the growing demands of an information society.
With the easily accessible Internet, residents in Taipei are able to search for any information on any device at any time. This not only improves people's working efficiency, but also increases the whole society's competitive edge.

中譯

題目	網路的優點
主題句	網路已是很先進又普遍的工具,社會大眾極度地依賴網路做日常溝通。
實例	比方說,台北市政府就已建設了無線網路,以因應日益增長的資訊社會需求。有了便利的網路之後,台北市的居民就可以隨時隨地,使用各式裝置,都可以取得所需資訊。這不僅增加了人們工作的效率,也提升了整個社會的競爭優勢。

範例 2 以「名人事蹟」來當實例

> **Question** In order to succeed, people should be different from others.

Topic sentence:

A person should stand out from the crowd in this competitive job market full of talented people.

Example:

Many successful leaders think differently and tend to analyze issues in a more innovative and unconventional manner. **For example, Mark Zuckerberg, the chairman and CEO of the social network site Facebook, is not afraid of taking risks and always thinks how to create a product that is innovative, that breaks all the rules, that changes everything.** And eventually he creates a company that has revolutionized the Internet.

中譯

題目	人要與眾不同才會成功。
主題句	身處於充滿人才的競爭激烈的就業市場上,一個人要儘可能在團體中突顯自己。
實例	很多成功人士以不同的方式思考,並傾向使用創新和跳脫傳統的方式來分析議題。舉例來說,馬克‧扎克伯格,也就是社群網路 Factbook(臉書)的執行長,並不害怕冒險,且他總是思考著如何創作出一個創新、打破成規、又可以改變世界的產品。最後,他打造了一個顛覆傳統網路的公司。

Question Benefits of saving money for the future

Topic sentence:

Saving money is the best way to handle both the uncertainties of life as well as to reach our financial dreams.

Example:

For example, when one of my friends, Terry, lost his job during economic recession in 2008, it was his previous savings that helped him meet his financial obligations until he got back on his feet. Furthermore, Terry now starts to save for his future dream, since one of his life goals is to establish a garden restaurant after he retires. Thus strong financial backup is absolutely necessary. Terry's experience also makes me realize the importance of saving money for the rainy day.

中譯

題目　　預先存錢的好處

主題句　存錢是應付生活中不時之需與實現未來夢想的最佳方式。

實例　　比方說，我的一個朋友，泰瑞，在 2008 年經濟蕭條時間失業，幸好是他有預備存款，讓他在重新振作起來之前可以先支付生活開支。此外，泰瑞現在也開始為他將來的夢想存款準備。他人生夢想之一是在退休後可開一間花園餐廳。因此，要有財務做後盾是絕對必要的。泰瑞的經驗讓我瞭解到未雨綢繆的重要性。

Question What can grandparents teach young people?

Topic sentence:

Grandparents possess years' worth of wisdom and experience that are worth passing on to the young generation, since they've gone through various challenges.

Example:

For instance, I used to hate having to learn about history in schoolbooks and from old paintings, but I found it more interesting to learn from grandparents who actually lived it. I learned from them what it was like to grow up during World War II. Their personal stories are much easier for me to remember than lists of names and dates from textbooks. Their sharing not only makes me realize how the life they've been through was different from my childhood, but also helps me score higher on history exams.

中譯

題目	祖父母可以教年輕人什麼？
主題句	祖父母因親身體驗過各種挑戰，因此他們擁有數年的生活智慧與經驗，都是值得傳給年輕一代的。
實例	比方說，我曾經很討厭從課本上看舊圖片來學歷史，但我就覺得聽親身體驗過的祖父母來講歷史就很有趣。我從他們的講述瞭解到生活在二戰時期是什麼樣子。對我來說，他們的個人故事比課本中所列的人名和日期更容易記憶。他們的分享不僅讓我瞭解到他們的生活和我的有何不同，也讓我的歷史考試分數更高了。

Question A city worth visiting in your country

Topic sentence:

Taipei is one of Asia's most exciting cities.

Example:

Taipei is the center of political, commercial and cultural activities in Taiwan. It is famous for its bustling business centers, energetic nightlife and colorful marketplaces. **For example, the well-known Taipei 101 Building is one of the tallest buildings in the world and the shopping center inside it is equally fantastic! In addition, night markets are my favorite places for traditional Taiwanese food.** The combination of both modern and traditional sides makes Taipei a really attractive city.

中譯

題目　你國家值得參觀的都市

主題句　台北是亞洲最有趣的都市之一。

實例　台北是台灣的政治、經濟和文化活動的中心。台北有名的是熙來攘往的商務中心、活躍的夜生活和多彩多姿的夜市。舉例來說，知名的台北 101 大樓是世界最高樓之一，裡面的購物中心也是同等華麗。此外，夜市是我最喜歡享用傳統美食的地方。先進與傳統兩面的結合讓台北變成一個迷人的都市。

EXERCISE 寫作練習

請在第 178 頁的 5 個範例寫作練習中，接續你所發揮的主題句，延伸寫出細節例證。

五、結論段落 (Conclusion)

❶ 結論的必要元素

一篇文章的最後部份就是結論段落了。結論段的作用，是將自己的立場與上述兩個或三個意見加以重申強調，以便收尾。因此在結論段落內，並不適合再發展寫出其他新的點子。通常結論段可能包括以下幾個元素：

A 將主要論點 (thesis statement) 再重述一次，但最好換句話說，使用不同的用字與表達方式。

B 將主題句 (topic sentences) 要點再重述一次。

C 若行有餘力，可再加入自己的預測，提供解決辦法等。但若時間不足，此句可以省去。

❷ 引出結論的用語

較常見用來引出結論段的用語包括：

- **In sum,**
- **In brief,**
- **To conclude,**
- **On the whole,**
- **In short,**
- **In conclusion,**
- **To summarize,**
- **In the end,**
- **All in all,**
- **To sum up,**

考官讀者看到這些用語出現，便會知道作者意見已論述完畢，因此要下結論了。我們使用之前討論過的一則題目來當例子：

Thesis statement:

I hold the belief that <u>working in the office</u> is more beneficial than working at home.

Topic sentence #1	**First of all**, working in the office enables employees to focus entirely on their tasks.
Topic sentence #2	**Secondly**, working in the office makes coworkers get involved in discussion more easily.
Topic sentence #3	**In contrast**, people working from home might find various distractions challenging to their productivity.

針對此題目的 thesis statement 與三個 topic sentences 所引出的結論，便可以寫為：

Conclusion 結論	To conclude, I assert working in the office is better than working at home alone. Employees generally perform better in a productive workplace, and they are able to have face-to-face interaction and exchange creative ideas with colleagues. Working at home might not be a brilliant idea for people who are not self-motivated enough. 結論是，我確信在辦公室工作比單獨在家工作要好。一般來說員工在有生產力的環境之下表現會較好，且他們可以跟同事面對面溝通，並交換有創意的點子。在家工作的話，對自我要求不高的人來說，可能不會是個理想的主意。

接下來，請參考另外五組結論段的撰寫範例。

3 📝 **五個範例**

Question Do you agree or disagree with this statement? People who cannot accept others' criticism cannot succeed in group working.

Thesis statement:

I hold the belief that people who adopt direct but legitimate criticism have better chances to succeed in group working.

Topic sentence #1	**First**, accepting constructive criticism allows workers to analyze an issue more objectively, instead of focusing on a single standpoint.
Topic sentence #2	**Further**, workers usually find working with flexible colleagues more pleasant, and thus they are willing to contribute more creative ideas.
Topic sentence #3	**However**, people who are too stubborn to open to disapprovals might miss the opportunity to gain new insights.
Conclusion	**In sum, I hold that people who are willing to accept criticism could achieve more in a team, since they gain valuable opportunities to expose themselves to new ideas, and win respect from colleagues. People who refuse to hear disagreement might lose the chances to experience such benefits.**

中譯

題目	你同意此觀點嗎？無法接受批評的人在團體內工作無法成功。
論點句	我認為可以接受直接且合理批評的人在團體內較容易成功。
主題句 #1	首先，接受具建設性的批評讓員工可以更客觀地分析事情，而非僅從單方面來思考。
主題句 #2	接著，員工通常會覺得跟有彈性的同事共事較愉快，也因此他們也較願意貢獻更多有創意的點子。
主題句 #3	然而，過於固執而不願意聽相反意見的人，可能會失去學習到新見解的機會。
結論	因此，我認為可以接受他人批評的人在團體內可以表現更好，因為他們有吸取不同意見的機會，且會得到同事的尊重。拒絕聽不同意見的人可能會失去這些好處。

範例 2

> **Question** Do you think children should spend time studying and playing or helping with the house chores?

Thesis statement:

In my opinion, children should balance their time doing both.

Topic sentence #1	**To begin with**, acquiring knowledge and interacting with classmates in school are major obligations for children.
Topic sentence #2	**At the same time**, assisting parents with household chores helps children to develop the sense of responsibility.
Conclusion	**To sum up, I believe that in order to help children acquire necessary abilities to perform well at school as well as getting the sense of responsibility, spending time studying and having fun at school and helping parents with household chores are equally essential.**

中譯

題目	你認為小孩應該花時間讀書和玩樂，還是應該幫忙家務呢？
論點句	在我看來，小孩應該在這兩者間取得平衡。
主題句 #1	首先，在校習得知識和跟同學互動，本是小孩的主要活動。
主題句 #2	同時，協助父母做家事也可以培養小孩的責任感。
結論	因此結論是，我認為為了讓小孩同時在校可習得該有的技能，也培養責任感，花時間在讀書和玩樂上，與花時間幫忙家務是同等重要。

Question Do you think, in order to succeed, a person should be more like others or be different from everyone else?

Thesis statement:

I think an individual should differentiate himself from others and brings his unique talents to the table.

Topic sentence #1	**First of all**, a person is most likely to achieve more if he uses his talents to the fullest extent.
Topic sentence #2	**Next**, a person should stand out from the crowd in today's competitive job market full of talented people.
Topic sentence #3	**In contrast**, a conservative person who just wants to follow others' steps might miss the opportunity to embrace new experience.
Conclusion	**In brief, I am a firm believer that if a person wants to one-up others, he must realize his own potential, dare to be different, and bold enough to think untraditionally.**

中譯

題目句	你認為,一個人要成功,應該要跟大家一樣就好,還是要與眾不同?
論點	我認為一個人應將自己跟他人區隔開,並發揮自己的才能。
主題句 #1	首先,若人可以全然發揮自己的長才,才較容易成就更多。
主題句 #2	再者,在今日充滿人才的競爭就業市場上,人更應該從人群中勝出。
主題句 #3	相反地,若過於保守的人只想要跟隨別人的腳步,那他有可能就會失去接觸新經驗的機會了。
結論	簡言之,我堅信若一個人想略勝他人一籌,他便要發揮自己的潛能,勇敢地展現與眾不同之處,並勇於以非傳統的方式思考。

Question Why do you choose to study abroad?

Thesis statement:
I choose to study in the U.S. because such an experience can bring more benefits not only for myself, but also for my home country.

Topic sentence #1	**To begin with**, I want to master my English ability in the US, the 100% English-speaking environment.
Topic sentence #2	**And that is not all.** I'd also like to explore more about American culture and actually experience it.
Topic sentence #3	**Finally**, my ultimate goal is to enhance my professional knowledge so I can make contributions to Taiwanese people.
Conclusion	**In conclusion, I've been planning to study in the US, as I want to sharpen my English skills, experience American culture myself, and in the long run, I want to make contributions to my homeland.**

中譯

題目	你為何選擇出國留學?
論點句	我選擇去美國留學,因為這樣的機會可以為我自己和我的國家帶來更多好處。
主題句 #1	首先,我想要在美國,百分之百英語系的國家,增強我的英文能力。
主題句 #2	還不止這樣。我也想探索更多美國文化,並親身去體驗。
主題句 #3	最後,我最終是想加強我的專業技能,也才能回國對台灣人做出些貢獻。
結論	因此結論是,我已規劃要去美國唸書,因為我想要精進我的英文能力,親自體驗美國文化,和長遠地來看,要對自己的國家作出貢獻。

Question Do you think people should take risks or experience new things when they are young or when they are older?

Thesis statement:

I personally hold the belief that people ought to pursue challenges and embrace more experience when they are still young.

Topic sentence #1	**On one hand**, young people are energetic and flexible and such characteristics enable them to adapt to risks or recover from setbacks without a hitch.
Topic sentence #2	**On the other hand**, seasoned adults also have rights to pursue dreams, of course. However, they are more likely to be held back by certain concerns.
Conclusion	**In sum, I strongly believe that young people should take risks and learn valuable lessons from difficulties, as they are passionate about life and energetic. Older people could also seek new challenges, but they might concern more about other factors than their own benefits.**

中譯

題目	你認為人們應該趁年輕的時候就去冒險或體驗新事物，還是要等老一點再說？
論點句	我個人是認為，人們應該趁年輕的時候去追求挑戰，並擁抱新的機會。
主題句 #1	一方面來說，年輕人有活力又有彈性，這樣的特質讓他們可以適應挑戰並很快地從挫折中復原。
主題句 #2	另一方面來看，有經驗的成人當然也是有權力追求夢想。但他們可能比較容易受到其他事務的牽絆。
結論	總而言之，我強烈認為年輕人應該要去冒險，並從困難中學習寶貴的經驗，正因為他們對生命充滿熱情又精力十足。年長者也可以尋求新的挑戰，但他們可能會考慮到其他的因素而不僅是自己的利益。

EXERCISE 寫作練習

請在第 178 頁的 5 個範例寫作練習中，延伸寫出結論。

UNIT 4 ▶ 實務寫作

──綜合範文 10 篇

在討論過開場段落，每段主題句、舉例和結論段落的寫法之後，最重要的自然就是要將這些片段組合起來，成為一篇完整的文章了。

以下十篇的主題包括：社會、生活、金錢、教育、科技、商業……等議題，是不管哪種類型的寫作考試都常考的主題。每篇段落也都套用了前面章節所述的Organization 架構，方便同學比對參考。

再者，下列範文字數都在 280 字上下，若有些寫作考試要求字數較少（150 字或180 字左右），則可以自行參考增減。選取適用同學本身情況的文句來學習模仿即可。

最後，再度提醒同學，所有題目都沒有標準答案。參考範文是學習的過程之一，但最重要的是，要親自分析題目、找資料、練文字，提筆寫出專屬於自己的一篇文章喔！

Q1 Discuss why nowadays young people are better able to make decisions in their own lives.

It is generally considered that in the past young people were less actively involved in making their own decisions since their parents were the people to make plans. But, young people nowadays are better able to proactively participate in the decision making process and set their own goals. I think this is the result of the availability of information and encouragement from adults.

First of all, a huge amount of diversified information today stimulates young people to form their own judgment. In the past, young people were not exposed to as much information as young people are nowadays, so they lacked sufficient information to support their decisions. On the contrary, young people today do have access to information through various channels, such as news, TV programs, and even the Internet. My 20-year-old brother, for example, spends more time on the Internet searching for solutions to his own problems rather than consulting my parents for suggestions. Handy information enables young people to form their opinions independently.

More significantly, nowadays a lot of open-minded adults encourage young people to exercise their judgement and make their own decisions. For example, one of my supervisors always urges young team members to be bold enough to generate original ideas and make appropriate decisions. He is a firm believer that young adults are mature enough to be responsible for whatever decisions they have made. Therefore, with full support from adults, young people nowadays have more freedom to decide what they want to achieve.

To summarize, I think that young people today do have more opportunity to exercise their judgement, as they are exposed to more information and resources and get support from their seniors.

(278 words)

問題：討論現在年輕人較能夠為自己的人生做決定的原因。

一般來說，我們認為過去的年輕人較不積極做出自己的決定，因為他們的父母才是制定計劃的人。然而，現今的年輕人比較能夠主動地參與決定以及設定自己的目標。我認為這是資訊發達與來自大人鼓勵的結果。

首先，今日有大量的多元化資訊激發年輕人運用自己的判斷力。在過去，年輕人不比現在的年輕人一樣可接觸到那麼多的資訊，因此缺乏充分的資訊來支持他們的決定。相反的，現在的年輕人透過許多不同的管道取得資訊，像是新聞、電視節目、甚至是網路。舉例而言，我二十歲的弟弟花很多的時間，在網路上為他所遇到的問題找答案，而不是向父母尋求建議。隨手可得的資訊讓年輕人可以獨立地形成自己的意見。

更重要的是，現在有許多思想較開放的成年人，鼓勵年輕人運用自己的判斷力並做出自己的決定。舉例來說，我有一個主管總是鼓勵年輕的團隊成員，大膽地提出自己原創的概念並做出適當的決策。他堅信年輕的成人夠成熟可以為他們做出的所有決定負責。因此，有了來自成人的全力支援，現在的年輕人可以得到更大的自由來決定他們想達成的成就。

總而言之，我認為現在的年輕人有更多的機會可以執行他的判斷力，因為他們暴露在更多的資訊以及資源中，並從較年長者身上得到完整的支持。

文章結構分析

開場段落	It is generally considered that in the past young people were less actively involved in making their own decisions since their parents were the people to make plans. But, young people nowadays are better able to proactively participate in the decision making process and set their own goals. I think this is the result of the availability of information and encouragement from adults.	第 1 句：說明 第 2 句：引題 第 3 句：表態
文章主體 **Idea 1**	First of all, a huge amount of diversified information today stimulates young people to form their own judgment. In the past, young people were not exposed to as much information as young people are nowadays, so they lacked sufficient information to support their decisions. On the contrary, young people today do have access to information through various channels, such as news, TV programs, and even the Internet. My 20-year-old brother, for example, spends more time on the Internet searching for solutions to his own problems rather than consulting my parents for suggestions. Handy information enables young people to form their opinions independently.	主題句 1 細節例證
文章主體 **Idea 2**	More significantly, nowadays a lot of open-minded adults encourage young people to exercise their judgement and make their own decisions. For example, one of my supervisors always urges young team members to be bold enough to generate original ideas and make appropriate decisions. He is a firm believer that young adults are mature enough to be responsible for whatever decisions they have made. Therefore, with full support from adults, young people nowadays have more freedom to decide what they want to achieve.	主題句 2 細節例證
結論段落	To summarize, I [引出結論段用語] oday do have more opportunity to exercise their judgement, as they are exposed to more information and resources and get support from their seniors.	重述主要論點

Q2 **Advertising is a waste of time and money because customers already know what they want. Agree or disagree?**

Is advertising a waste of time and money, since nowadays most consumers are aware of what they need to purchase already? I hold that the real value and effectiveness of advertising really depend on what industry and product type we are talking about. Let me elaborate further below.

To begin with, advertising does play an important role in promoting commodities or services. Advertising is one of the most direct ways to communicate with a target audience and encourage customers to purchase products. For example, once I couldn't make up my mind where to spend my vacation. Not until I saw an advertisement in the Travel Magazine describing how enjoyable a vacation in Florida could be did I decide to spend a week there. Thanks to all sorts of advertisements appearing in people's daily life, people are well-informed about what products or services are available on the market. In this situation, advertising is effective and should not be considered a waste of money and time.

However, the effectiveness of advertising might be less apparent for specific industries. For example, I used to work at Smart-Tech Systems, a network integration company. Most of the company's target clients were major IT firms and they knew exactly what solution would meet their needs already. Their purchasing decision was not based on whether the advertisement was appealing or not. In this case, spending efforts and resources on advertising Smart-Tech's specific system solutions was not an effective strategy.

In sum, advertising is crucial and necessary for some general products and services, but is probably not that worthwhile for specific industries. In order to be more profitable, companies should focus on the most effective advertising strategy to promote products.

(282 words)

Q2 範文中譯

問題：你是否同意此觀點：登廣告是浪費錢又浪費時間，因為客戶早就知道自己要買什麼產品了。

在現代，大多數的消費者都已經知道自己想購買的是什麼產品了，所以廣告真的只是浪費時間與金錢嗎？我認為廣告的實際價值與有效性端視我們討論的產業以及產品類型為何而定。讓我在下方進一步地說明。

首先，廣告確實在促銷商品或服務中扮演了重要的角色。廣告是與目標客群交流的最直接方法，並鼓勵消費者購買產品。舉例而言，有一次我無法決定要在哪裡度假，一直到我看到旅遊雜誌上的廣告，雜誌中描述了佛羅里達的假期有多好玩，我才決定去佛羅里達度假一週。所幸在日常的生活中有各式各樣的廣告，人們才可得到豐富的資訊，了解市場上有哪些產品或服務可供選擇。在這種情況下，廣告是有效的，且不應該被認為是浪費時間與金錢。

然而，廣告的效用在特定產業中可能比較不明顯。舉例而言，我以前在 Smart-Tech 系統公司工作，那是一間網路整合公司。公司大多數的目標客戶都是大型的 IT 公司，而且他們完全知道要採用何種解決方案來滿足他們的需求了。他們的採購決策並不會受到廣告是否吸引人的影響。在此情況下，花費心力與資源在推廣 Smart-Tech 的特定解決方案上，可能不是有效的策略。

總而言之，在一些通用產品及服務上，廣告是重要且必須的，但在特定產業中可能就不是那麼必要。為了得到更為豐厚的利潤，公司必須要著重於最適當的廣告策略來推廣產品。

文章結構分析

開場段落	Is advertising a waste of time and money, since nowadays most consumers are aware of what they need to purchase already? I hold that the real value and effectiveness of advertising really depend on what industry and product type we are talking about. Let me elaborate further below.	← 引題 ← 表態
文章主體 **Idea 1**	To begin with, advertising does play an important role in promoting commodities or services. Advertising is one of the most direct ways to communicate with a target audience and encourage customers to purchase products. For example, once I couldn't make up my mind where to spend my vacation. Not until I saw an advertisement in the Travel Magazine describing how enjoyable a vacation in Florida could be did I decide to spend a week there. Thanks to all sorts of advertisements appearing in people's daily life, people are well-informed about what products or services are available on the market. In this situation, advertising is effective and should not be considered a waste of money and time.	← 主題句 1 ─ 細節例證
文章主體 **Idea 2**	However, the effectiveness of advertising might be less apparent for specific industries. For example, I used to work at Smart-Tech Systems, a network integration company. Most of the company's target clients were major IT firms and they knew exactly what solution would meet their needs already. Their purchasing decision was not based on whether the advertisement was appealing or not. In this case, spending efforts and resources on advertising Smart-Tech's specific system solutions was not an effective strategy.	← 主題句 2 ─ 細節例證
結論段落	In sum, advertising is crucial and necessary for some general products and services, but is probably not that worthwhile for specific industries. In order to be more profitable, companies should focus on the most effective advertising strategy to promote products.	─ 重述主要論點

Financial management is a significant part of people's life, since it can determine what we can do and where we can go. Different views thus exist about whether people should spend money on short-term pleasure, such as traveling and vacations, or save money for the future. I personally like to establish budget plans for both.

On the one hand, spending money on traveling and vacations is worthwhile because traveling increases our knowledge and widens our perspective. Having lived in Taiwan for the past three decades, I've realized the importance of opening my mind and experience life in different ways. For example, I always have crazy schedules, and whenever I need a break, I allocate some budget and go traveling. Whether it's a long vacation or just a weekend getaway, discovering different ways to get by in life is really interesting, and it boosts my energy to keep moving forward.

On the other hand, saving money is the best way to handle both the uncertainties of life as well as to reach our financial dreams. For example, when one of my friends, Terry, lost his job during the economic recession in 2008, it was his previous savings that helped him meet his financial obligations until he got back on his feet. Furthermore, Terry has now started to save for his future, since one of his life goals is to establish a garden restaurant after he retires. Thus, strong financial backup is absolutely necessary. Terry's experience also makes me realize the importance of saving money for a rainy day.

In sum, people should carefully manage their finances and spend their money not only on traveling and vacations, but also save for the future. I do believe that spending money traveling is worthwhile, and saving money for a rainy day is equally essential.

(300 words)

問題：你想花錢在旅遊度假上，還是要存起來未來使用呢？

金錢管理是人們生活中重要的一環，因為金錢可以影響到我們能做的事情還有可以去的地方。因此，對於人們是否應該花錢在追求短期的享樂上，像是旅行與假期，還是存錢以待日後使用這個議題，存在不同的觀點。我個人會想要同時為兩者都編列預算。

一方面，把錢花在旅行以及假期上是很值得的，因為旅行可以增加我們的知識並增廣我們的見聞。在台灣生活了三十年，我發現到打開心胸以及以不同方式體驗生活的重要性。舉例來說，我總是非常地忙碌，而當我需要喘口氣時，我就會分配一些預算出發去旅行。可能是長期旅行或僅是週末小旅行，探索過生活的不同方式真的相當有趣，而且可以增強你繼續向前的能量。

另一方面，存錢是處理生活中不確定性還有達成我們財務夢想的最佳方法。好比說，當我的一個朋友，泰瑞，在 2008 年經濟衰退期丟了工作，就是因為有先前的存款，他才能支付生活所需一直到他重新振作起來找到工作為止。甚至，泰瑞現在開始為了未來的夢想儲蓄，因為他人生的目標之一就是要在退休後開一間花園餐廳。因此，健全強大的財務後盾是絕對必須的。泰瑞的經驗也讓我了解到未雨綢繆需要存錢的重要性。

總而言之，人們應該小心管理自己的財務，不要只是花在旅行及假期上，也要為了未來做準備。我深信把錢花在旅行上是值得的，而未雨綢繆先存錢也一樣的重要。

文章結構分析

開場段落	Financial management is a significant part of people's life, since it can determine what we can do and where we can go. Different views thus exist about whether people should spend money on short-term pleasure, such as traveling and vacations, or save money for the future. I personally like to establish budget plans for both.	第 1 句：說明 第 2 句：引題 第 3 句：表態
文章主體 **Idea 1**	On the one hand, spending money on traveling and vacations is worthwhile because traveling increases our knowledge and widens our perspective. Having lived in Taiwan for the past three decades, I've realized the importance of opening my mind and experience life in different ways. For example, I always have crazy schedules, and whenever I need a break, I allocate some budget and go traveling. Whether it's a long vacation or just a weekend getaway, discovering different ways to get by in life is really interesting, and it boosts my energy to keep moving forward.	主題句 1 細節例證
文章主體 **Idea 2**	On the other hand, saving money is the best way to handle both the uncertainties of life as well as to reach our financial dreams. For example, when one of my friends, Terry, lost his job during the economic recession in 2008, it was his previous savings that helped him meet his financial obligations until he got back on his feet. Furthermore, Terry has now started to save for his future, since one of his life goals is to establish a garden restaurant after he retires. Thus, strong financial backup is absolutely necessary. Terry's experience also makes me realize the importance of saving money for a rainy day.	主題句 2 細節例證
結論段落	In sum, people should carefully manage their finances and spend their money not only on traveling and vacations, but also save for the future. I do believe that spending money traveling is worthwhile, and saving money for a rainy day is equally essential.	重述主要論點

Do you prefer to use your own knowledge and experience to solve problems or to ask other people for advice?

Some people prefer to solve problems by using their own knowledge and experience, while others may want to get advice from their friends or family members. In my own opinion, it really depends on what kind of problems I encounter. Let me explain further below.

First of all, I evaluate whether the problem I encounter can be solved through my own knowledge or past experience. If I happened to deal with similar situations in the past, I definitely make good use of my problem-solving skills. For example, when I presented a science project in front of the class for the first time in high school, I felt extremely nervous. Then I figured out ways to control my anxiety, so now whenever I need to speak in front of a group, I just take it easy. This example shows that I can learn a valuable lesson from my own experience.

However, sometimes I think asking for advice from other people might be a more direct way to solve problems. Other people share their valuable experience with me, so this prevents me from going in the wrong direction and saves me precious time. For instance, at first I had little understanding of what the TOEIC exam is all about. Instead of spending time trying to figure out all the exam strategies by myself, I discussed my problem with seasoned teachers and eventually came up with some good test strategies to score high on this exam.

After all, relying on my own experience and asking for advice are both good ways to get problems solved. I try to make good use of my knowledge and experience to analyze the situation, and at the same time, I also consult with others for constructive suggestions. I believe the combination of these two methods can help me deal with problems in a more effective manner.

(310 words)

問題：你喜歡以自己的知識和經驗來解決問題，還是請別人給意見？

有些人喜歡利用自身的知識以及經驗解決問題，而有些人可能想要得到朋友或家人的意見。在我看來，這要端看我所遇到的問題是何種類型。讓我在下方進一步地說明。

首先，我會先評估我所遇到的問題是否可以靠自己的知識或過去的經驗來解決。若我過去剛好處理過類似的狀況，我絕對會想要善用我解決問題的能力。舉例來說，當我在高中第一次在全班面前報告科學專案時，我感到極度地緊張。然後，我找到方法控制我的焦慮感，所以之後當我要在一大群人前面發表意見時，我就能放輕鬆了。這個例子顯示出我可以從自己的經驗中學到寶貴的一課。

然而，有時候我覺得詢問其他人的意見可能可以更直接地解決我的問題。其他人會跟我分享他們寶貴的經驗，這樣可以讓我不會走上錯誤的方向，並且省下寶貴的時間。例如，一開始我對多益測驗所知不多，與其花時間試著要靠自己找出考試策略，我會跟經驗豐富的老師討論然後想出好的考試策略，以在這次考試中得到高分。

畢竟，依賴我自己的經驗還有尋求他人的意見，都是解決問題的好方法。我試著善加利用我的知識與經驗來分析狀況，同時，我也會向他人請教有建設性的意見。我認為結合這兩個方法可以協助我以更有效的方式處理問題。

文章結構分析

開場段落	Some people prefer to solve problems by using their own knowledge and experience, while others may want to get advice from their friends or family members. In my own opinion, it really depends on what kind of problems I encounter. Let me explain further below.	說明、引題 / 表態
文章主體 Idea 1	First of all, I evaluate whether the problem I encounter can be solved through my own knowledge or past experience. If I happened to deal with similar situations in the past, I definitely make good use of my problem-solving skills. For example, when I presented a science project in front of the class for the first time in high school, I felt extremely nervous. Then I figured out ways to control my anxiety, so now whenever I need to speak in front of a group, I just take it easy. This example shows that I can learn a valuable lesson from my own experience.	主題句 1 / 細節例證
文章主體 Idea 2	However, sometimes I think asking for advice from other people might be a more direct way to solve problems. Other people share their valuable experience with me, so this prevents me from going in the wrong direction and saves me precious time. For instance, at first I had little understanding of what the TOEIC exam is all about. Instead of spending time trying to figure out all the exam strategies by myself, I discussed my problem with seasoned teachers and eventually came up with some good test strategies to score high on this exam.	主題句 2 / 細節例證
結論段落	After all, relying on my own experience and asking for advice are both good ways to get problems solved. I try to make good use of my knowledge and experience to analyze the situation, and at the same time, I also consult with others for constructive suggestions. I believe the combination of these two methods can help me deal with problems in a more effective manner.	重述主要論點

Q5 **Do you think that people who try to acquire more than one skill are more likely to become successful than people who just focus on one skill?**

People all aspire to climb to the top of their respective professions, but in order to achieve this goal, do people need to acquire more than one skill or to concentrate entirely on just one competence? I hold that people should possess multiple skills to succeed. My reasons are as follows.

First of all, obtaining multiple skills enables people to expand their opportunities. I myself, for example, studied at National Taiwan University and majored in Computer Science. Not only did I take the required computer programming courses, but I also received lots of English training. When I worked in a hi-tech company, in addition to being responsible for promoting software products, I was also assigned by my supervisor to participate in major meetings with overseas vendors, because of my outstanding oral English ability. And I was promoted to the Asian Regional team two years later. Both my professional computer expertise and English skills allowed me to advance my career path more easily than other colleagues who possessed only one single skill.

In addition, people who have more than one skill are more likely to realize their full potential. One obvious example is that nowadays, many lawyers pursue two careers, practicing law and writing novels, particularly thrillers and mysteries. These lawyers provide legal services and want to fulfill their dream of writing novels as well. Best of all, they are able to put their own legal knowledge to use in their books. It is clear from this example that professional lawyers who also have sharp imagination and good writing skills can realize their potential by combining the two essential activities.

In sum, in order to succeed, I hold that various skills are indispensable, as multiple skills increase our chances to expand our career domain and realize our full potential.

(298 words)

問題：你認為擁有多樣技能的人，比僅擁有一樣技能的人更容易成功嗎？

人們都嚮往著要在自己專業領域中成功，為了達到此目標，人們需要取得一種以上的技能還是完全專注在一種職能上呢？我認為人們應該要擁有多種技能才會成功。我的理由如下。

首先，取得多種技能讓人們可以擴展更多的機會。舉例來說，我之前在國立台灣大學唸書，主修資訊工程。我不僅修必要的電腦程式編寫課程，我也接受大量的英語口說訓練。當我在 Hi-Tech 公司工作時，除了負責促銷軟體套裝，也因為我有卓越的英語口說能力，我才受到主管指派，參加世界供應商的重大會議。而且在兩年後，我受到拔擢進入亞洲區團隊工作。我的電腦專門知識以及英語能力，讓我能比其他只有一種單一技能的同事更輕鬆地在職業生涯的路徑上邁進。

此外，有一種以上能力的人們比較有可能發展他們所有的潛力。一個很明顯的例子就是，現在許多律師都都同時進行兩種工作，也就是從事法律相關工作以及寫小說，特別是驚悚與推理小說。律師們提供法律服務，但也想要滿足他們寫小說的夢想。最棒的是，他們可以將他們的法律知識用在故事中。從這個範例可以很清楚地看到，有銳利想像力以及好文筆的專業律師可以結合兩個重要技能來發展自己的潛力。

總而言之，為了成功，我支持有多種技能是不可或缺的，因為多種技能可以增加我們擴展職業領域的機會，並且實現所有潛力。

文章結構分析

段落	內容	說明
開場段落	People all aspire to climb to the top of their respective professions, but in order to achieve this goal, do people need to acquire more than one skill or to concentrate entirely on just one competence? I hold that people should possess multiple skills to succeed. My reasons are as follows.	← 說明、引題 ← 表態
文章主體 Idea 1	First of all, obtaining multiple skills enables people to expand their opportunities. I myself, for example, studied at National Taiwan University and majored in Computer Science. Not only did I take the required computer programming courses, but I also received lots of English training. When I worked in a hi-tech company, in addition to being responsible for promoting software products, I was also assigned by my supervisor to participate in major meetings with overseas vendors, because of my outstanding oral English ability. And I was promoted to the Asian Regional team two years later. Both my professional computer expertise and English skills allowed me to advance my career path more easily than other colleagues who possessed only one single skill.	← 主題句 1 細節例證
文章主體 Idea 2	In addition, people who have more than one skill are more likely to realize their full potential. One obvious example is that nowadays, many lawyers pursue two careers, practicing law and writing novels, particularly thrillers and mysteries. These lawyers provide legal services and want to fulfill their dream of writing novels as well. Best of all, they are able to put their own legal knowledge to use in their books. It is clear from this example that professional lawyers who also have sharp imagination and good writing skills can realize their potential by combining the two essential activities.	← 主題句 2 細節例證
結論段落	In sum, in order to succeed, I hold that various skills are indispensable, as multiple skills increase our chances to expand our career domain and realize our full potential.	重述主要論點

If I needed to suggest just one city for my foreign friends to visit, it would have to be Taipei. Not only is Taipei the place in which I was born, but it is also an international city worth visiting in Taiwan.

The first point I want to make is that Taipei is one of Asia's most exciting cities. Taipei is this island's center of political, commercial and cultural activities. It is famous for its bustling business centers, energetic nightlife and colorful marketplaces. For example, the well-known Taipei 101 Building is one of the tallest buildings in the world and the shopping center inside it is equally fantastic! In addition, night markets are a great place for traditional Taiwanese food. The combination of both modern and traditional aspects makes Taipei a really attractive city.

Second, Taipei is home to some of our most famous museums. The importance of these museums is that they put Taiwanese heritage on display. Visiting these museums would be a helpful introduction for what our country is all about. One must-visit museum in Taipei is the National Palace Museum, and it is the world's most extensive collections of Chinese art and antiquities.

Finally, I think Taipei is one of the most beautiful parts of the country. Taipei is a basin with two rivers running through it - the Tamsui and the Keelung - and it is surrounded by mountains. That makes for plenty of green space right in the center of the city. My favorite park is the Da An Forest Park. Like the name implies, the Da An Forest Park is dedicated first and foremost to trees although there is also lots of grassy space.

To summarize, I would recommend that my foreign friends spend some time in our capital city, because Taipei City is exciting, has museums worth visiting, and is attractive.

(308 words)

問題：請描述你國家值得參觀的都市。

若需要我提供國外朋友來訪城市的建議，我想我一定會推薦台北市。不只是因為我出生於台北，也因為台北是台灣值得拜訪的國際城市。

我想說的第一點是，台北是亞洲中最好玩的城市之一。台北是台灣的政治、商業以及文化活動的中心。它因為繁華的商業中心、充滿活力的夜生活，還有多采多姿的市集而知名。例如，廣為人知的台北 101 大樓就是世界最高的建築之一，裡面的購物中心也一樣棒！此外，夜市也因為有多種傳統台灣食物，而成為我最喜愛的地方。現代與傳統的結合讓台北市成為一個相當吸引人的城市。

第二，台北是好幾所知名博物館的發源地。這些博物館的重要性在於他們展示出台灣文化遺產。拜訪這些博物館是我們國家相關傳承最有幫助的介紹。一間位於台北的必訪博物館就是國立故宮博物院，它是世界上藏有最多中國藝術及文物的博物館。

最後，我認為台北是這個國家中最美的地方。台北是一個盆地，有兩條河穿越其中——淡水和與基隆河——而且周圍有群山環繞。這讓台北的市中心有大量的綠地。我最喜歡的地方是大安森林公園。正如其名，雖然留有大片的草地，但是大安森林公園最主要是種了很多樹木。

總結來說，我會向我的國外朋友建議花點時間在我們的首都台北市逛逛，因為台北市很好玩，有值得拜訪的博物館而且很吸引人。

文章結構分析

段落	內容	說明
開場段落	If I needed to suggest just one city for my foreign friends to visit, it would have to be Taipei. Not only is Taipei the place in which I was born, but it is also an international city worth visiting in Taiwan.	直接切入主題＋表態
文章主體 Idea 1	The first point I want to make is that Taipei is one of Asia's most exciting cities. Taipei is this island's center of political, commercial and cultural activities. It is famous for its bustling business centers, energetic nightlife and colorful marketplaces. For example, the well-known Taipei 101 Building is one of the tallest buildings in the world and the shopping center inside it is equally fantastic! In addition, night markets are a great place for traditional Taiwanese food. The combination of both modern and traditional aspects makes Taipei a really attractive city.	主題句 1 / 細節例證
文章主體 Idea 2	Second, Taipei is home to some of our most famous museums. The importance of these museums is that they put Taiwanese heritage on display. Visiting these museums would be a helpful introduction for what our country is all about. One must-visit museum in Taipei is the National Palace Museum, and it is the world's most extensive collections of Chinese art and antiquities.	主題句 2 / 細節例證
文章主體 Idea 3	Finally, I think Taipei is one of the most beautiful parts of the country. Taipei is a basin with two rivers running through it - the Tamsui and the Keelung - and it is surrounded by mountains. That makes for plenty of green space right in the center of the city. My favorite park is the Da An Forest Park. Like the name implies, the Da An Forest Park is dedicated first and foremost to trees although there is also lots of grassy space.	主題句 3 / 細節例證
結論段落	To summarize, I would recommend that my foreign friends spend some time in our capital city, because Taipei City is exciting, has museums worth visiting, and is attractive.	重述主要論點

Q7 The Internet has changed the way people communicate. Discuss some advantages of the Internet.

Nowadays, no one can deny the significance of the Internet. The Internet has made this world a global village. Some people might focus on the downsides that the Internet brings, say the security issues. Still, I think that the advantages of the Internet outnumber the disadvantages.

First of all, the Internet is an excellent tool for communication. With the advent of the Internet, our earth has attained a size of a global village. An obvious example is that now I can communicate in a fraction of a second with my friends who are sitting on the other side of the world. There are also plenty of messenger services. With the help of such services, it has become very easy to establish a kind of global friendship where I can share my thoughts, and explore other cultures.

And that is not all. I think easy access to information is probably the biggest advantage of the Internet. Any kind of information on any topic under the sun is available on the Internet. For example, with search engines like Google and Yahoo I can find almost any type of data on almost any kind of subject that I am looking for. In addition, teachers in my university also give us assignments that require research on the Internet. We as students use the Internet for gathering resources as well.

Finally, I like all the services on the Internet, such as online banking, job seeking, purchasing tickets for my favorite movies, and hotel reservations. For instance, after I graduate next year I plan to use an online job bank as my major job searching tool.

To conclude, the Internet provides us with good communications, lots of information, and convenient services to make our lives easier. I just cannot imagine how I could live without the Internet.

(301 words)

Q7 範文中譯

問題：網路已改變人們溝通的方式了。請討論網路所帶來的好處。

在現代，沒有人可以否認網路的重要性。網路讓這個世界成為地球村。有些人可能會強調網路帶來負面影響，像是安全性的疑慮。但我還是認為網路帶來的優點遠勝缺點。

首先，網路是溝通所需的必備工具。透過電腦網路時代的來臨，我們的地球已經達成了某種形式的地球村。一個很明顯的例子就是現在我可以在不到一秒的時間內，就跟位於世界另一端的朋友通訊。網路上也有提供許多訊息服務。在這些服務的協助下，讓建立全球性友誼變得相當容易，我可以在網路上分享我的想法，也可以探索其他的文化。

還不只這些，我認為資訊取得可能是網路上可提供的最大優點。世上所有主題相關的任何資訊都可以在網路上取得，比方說像是 Google 以及 Yahoo! 的搜尋引擎。我幾乎可以找到我所搜尋的所有主題類型的相關資料。此外，我大學的老師也指派給我們需要在網路上做的研究。當學生的我們也可以使用網路收集資源。

最後，我喜歡所有網路上的服務，像是線上的銀行業務、線上找工作、買我喜歡的電影票、還有飯店訂房等。例如，在我畢業的隔年，我計劃使用線上工作銀行作為我主要的工作搜尋工具。

綜上所述，網路提供我們良好的通訊、大量資訊、以及便利的服務，讓我們的生活更為簡單。我就是無法想像沒有網路的生活。

文章結構分析

段落	內容	分析
開場段落	Nowadays, no one can deny the significance of the Internet. The Internet has made this world a global village. Some people might focus on the downsides that the Internet brings, say the security issues. Still, I think that the advantages of the Internet outnumber the disadvantages.	第 1 句：說明 第 2 句：引題 第 3 句：表態
文章主體 Idea 1	First of all, the Internet is an excellent tool for communication. With the advent of the Internet, our earth has attained a size of a global village. An obvious example is that now I can communicate in a fraction of a second with my friends who are sitting on the other side of the world. There are also plenty of messenger services. With the help of such services, it has become very easy to establish a kind of global friendship where I can share my thoughts, and explore other cultures.	主題句 1 細節例證
文章主體 Idea 2	And that is not all. I think easy access to information is probably the biggest advantage of the Internet. Any kind of information on any topic under the sun is available on the Internet. For example, with search engines like Google and Yahoo! I can find almost any type of data on almost any kind of subject that I am looking for. In addition, teachers in my university also give us assignments that require research on the Internet. We as students use the Internet for gathering resources as well.	主題句 2 細節例證
文章主體 Idea 3	Finally, I like all the services on the Internet, such as online banking, job seeking, purchasing tickets for my favorite movies, and hotel reservations. For instance, after I graduate next year I plan to use an online job bank as my major job searching tool.	主題句 3 細節例證
結論段落	To conclude, the Internet provides us with good communications, lots of information, and convenient services to make our lives easier. I just cannot imagine how I could live without the Internet.	重述主要論點

Q8 **Should the government focus more on improving the Internet or the public transportation system?**

Most countries in today's competitive world are trying hard to come up with development strategies, such as installing a complete Internet network for people to access or improving public transportation. This raises the issue of whether the government should focus more on improving Internet connections or expanding the local transportation network. I hold that the government should balance resources and efforts equally between the two.

First of all, the Internet is an essential tool that people depend heavily on for daily communication. In order to increase a country's competitive advantage, a complete Internet network is a must. For example, in Taipei our government has implemented a wireless Internet network in response to the growing demands of an information society. With easily accessible Internet, residents in Taipei are able to search for any information on any device at any time. This not only improves people's efficiency, but also increases the whole society's competitive edge.

At the same time, a well-developed public transportation system is essential for the prosperity of a society. Our government, for example, has devoted a great deal of time to building new MRT routes, and designing more advanced transit systems as well. Thanks to the complete and convenient public transportation system, Taipei has become an international city and a center of business and technological development.

Some people might argue that improving Internet access is more critical than building a transportation system, since people can take advantage of the web and work from home instead of commuting. This might be true for free-lance workers who can work wherever there is an Internet connection. However, there are still other occupations, such as sales representatives and freight carriers that require people to travel all the time. In this situation, a convenient public transportation system is necessary.

To sum up, I do support that the government should devote equal efforts to developing transportation systems and the Internet, as these two kinds of development are both beneficial to the general public.

(328 words)

問題：政府應將焦點放在改善網路還是大眾交通系統呢？

現代競爭世界中，有許多國家都努力地試著設計發展策略，像是安裝完整的網際網路提供民眾存取或是改善大眾運輸。這便產生了：政府是否應該注重在改善網路連線，還是擴展地方運輸？的議題。我認為政府應該平衡資源與精神在開發這兩者之間。

首先，網路已是如此現代化且普遍的工具，民眾相當依賴網路進行日常通訊。為了增加國家的競爭優勢，完整的網際網路是不可或缺的。舉例來說，我們的政府在台北佈署了無線網際網路，以反應資訊社會成長中的需求。有了可輕鬆取用的網路，居住在台北可以隨時使用各種裝置搜尋所有資訊。這不僅提升了民眾的效率，也增加了整體社會的競爭優勢。

同時，發展良好的大眾運輸系統在社會層面來看是不可或缺的。舉例來說，我們的政府花了大量的時間建造新的捷運路線，並也設計更多先進的交通系統。幸好有完整且便利的大眾運輸系統，台北才能成為國際都市還有商業以及技術發展的中心。

有些民眾可能會認為，改善網路存取比建造交通系統更為重要，因為人們可以利用網路在家工作，無需通勤。這對於能在任何有網路的地方工作的自由工作者來說或許是正確的。然而，也有些其他職業總是需要人外出旅行，像是銷售代表以及運輸業。在此情形中，便利的大眾運輸系統就是必要的。

綜上所述，我確實支持政府應該花費一樣的心力在發展交通系統以及網路上，因為這兩種發展都對一般大眾相當有益。

文章結構分析

開場段落	Most countries in today's competitive world are trying hard to come up with development strategies, such as installing a complete Internet network for people to access or improving public transportation. This raises the issue of whether the government should focus more on improving Internet connections or expanding the local transportation network. I hold that the government should balance resources and efforts equally between the two.	第 1 句：說明 第 2 句：引題 第 3 句：表態
文章主體 Idea 1	First of all, the Internet is an essential tool that people depend heavily on for daily communication. In order to increase a country's competitive advantage, a complete Internet network is a must. For example, in Taipei our government has implemented a wireless Internet network in response to the growing demands of an information society. With easily accessible Internet, residents in Taipei are able to search for any information on any device at any time. This not only improves people's efficiency, but also increases the whole society's competitive edge.	主題句 1 細節例證
文章主體 Idea 2	At the same time, a well-developed public transportation system is essential for the prosperity of a society. Our government, for example, has devoted a great deal of time to building new MRT routes, and designing more advanced transit systems as well. Thanks to the complete and convenient public transportation system, Taipei has become an international city and a center of business and technological development.	主題句 2 細節例證
文章主體 Idea 3	Some people might argue that improving Internet access is more critical than building a transportation system, since people can take advantage of the web and work from home instead of commuting. This might be true for free-lance workers who can work wherever there is an Internet connection. However, there are still other occupations, such as sales representatives and freight carriers that require people to travel all the time. In this situation, a convenient public transportation system is necessary.	反面論述 扭轉意見
結論段落	To sum up, I do support that the government should devote equal efforts to developing transportation systems and the Internet, as these two kinds of development are both beneficial to the general public.	重述主要論點

Q9 Children nowadays rely on technology too much. Do you think playing with simpler toys or playing outside with friends is better for children's development?

In this modern society, adults have easy access to all kinds of electronic devices and children are no exception. Children nowadays rely on technology so much that they have almost forgotten what it feels like to simply play with toys or enjoy outdoor activities with friends. I hold the belief that playing with toys or participating in outdoor activities is more beneficial for children's overall development. I'd like to discuss why further below.

To begin with, playing with simpler toys or participating in outdoor activities enables children to stay in good physical and mental health. I'd like to use my childhood experience as a good example. Usually after school or after I'd finished all my homework assignments, instead of offering me an iPad to play with and hoping to keep me quiet, my parents encouraged me to play tabletop games or compete in sports activities outdoors. Through all these meaningful exercises, not only am I now in good shape, but I also have a lot of discipline that enables me to perform well at school.

Some people might argue that technological devices have brought us a brand new way of communication, so children ought to familiarize themselves with new technology anyway. Such an idea seems somewhat reasonable in this competitive society. However, I still consider that children should learn to take advantage of new technologies ONLY after they are mature enough and can exercise their judgment to decide when and how to use electronic devices properly. If children start to use an iPad at an early age, say 7, they are more likely to encounter eyesight problems than other children who don't use iPads that much. In addition, some violent video games might do more harm than good to children's mental development.

To sum up, I certainly agree that children should play with simpler toys or play outside with friends so that they can stay in good health and develop exceptional personalities. Relying too much on new technological devices might limit their chances to boost their creativity or reduce their interests in exploring more exciting matters in the world.

(349 words)

問題：現今的小孩都過度依賴科技了。你認為玩簡單的玩具或去戶外活動對小孩的發展較好嗎？

在這個現代化的社會中，成人可以輕鬆取得所有類型的電子裝置，兒童也不例外。現在的兒童相當依賴科技，幾乎忘了玩玩具或是與朋友進行戶外活動的感覺。我認為玩玩具或是進行戶外活動對於兒童的整體發展較有益處。我想在下方進一步地討論。

首先，玩簡單的玩具或是參與戶外活動讓兒童能維持生理與心理上良好的健康狀況。我想用我的童年經驗來當實例。通常在放學後或是我完成所有的功課之後，父母不是給我 iPad 玩讓我保持安靜，反而是鼓勵我玩些桌上遊戲，或是去戶外從事競爭的運動活動。透過這些有意義的活動，我現在不僅身材很好，也建立穩定的情緒，讓我可以在學校表現更好。

有些人可能會認為科技裝置讓我們有嶄新的溝通方法，所以孩子們應該熟悉新的科技。這樣的想法在競爭的社會上某種程度而言是合理的。然而，我仍然認為兒童應該學習利用新的科技，「只有」在他們夠成熟，而且能有判斷力來決定何時以及如何正確的使用電子裝置的時候才恰當。若兒童在幼年早期的階段就使用 iPad，像是七歲就開始玩，這與其他不使用 iPad 那麼長時間的兒童相比，他們就比較會面臨到視力問題。此外，有些暴力電玩遊戲可能對兒童的心理發展造成弊多於利的影響。

總而言之，我相當支持兒童應該只玩玩具或者是跟朋友在戶外遊戲，這樣他們可以維持良好的健康狀況並且發展卓越的人格。過於依賴新的科技裝置可能會限制他們發展創意的機會，或是降低他們探索世界上更有趣事物的興趣。

文章結構分析

開場段落	In this modern society, adults have easy access to all kinds of electronic devices and children are no exception. Children nowadays rely on technology so much that they have almost forgotten what it feels like to simply play with toys or enjoy outdoor activities with friends. I hold the belief that playing with toys or participating in outdoor activities is more beneficial for children's overall development. I'd like to discuss why further below.	第 1 句：說明 第 2 句：引題 第 3 句：表態
文章主體 Idea 1	To begin with, playing with simpler toys or participating in outdoor activities enables children to stay in good physical and mental health. I'd like to use my childhood experience as a good example. Usually after school or after I'd finished all my homework assignments, instead of offering me an iPad to play with and hoping to keep me quiet, my parents encouraged me to play tabletop games or compete in sports activities outdoors. Through all these meaningful exercises, not only am I now in good shape, but I also have a lot of discipline that enables me to perform well at school.	主題句 1 細節例證
文章主體 Idea 2	Some people might argue that technological devices have brought us a brand new way of communication, so children ought to familiarize themselves with new technology anyway. Such an idea seems somewhat reasonable in this competitive society. However, I still consider that children should learn to take advantage of new technologies ONLY after they are mature enough and can exercise their judgment to decide when and how to use electronic devices properly. If children start to use an iPad at an early age, say 7, they are more likely to encounter eyesight problems than other children who don't use iPads that much. In addition, some violent video games might do more harm than good to children's mental development.	反面論述 扭轉意見
結論段落	To sum up, I certainly agree that children should play with simpler toys or play outside with friends so that they can stay in good health and develop exceptional personalities. Relying too much on new technological devices might limit their chances to boost their creativity or reduce their interests in exploring more exciting matters in the world.	重述主要論點

Q10 Do you prefer to work at home using computers or telephones or work in an office?

I happened to read in an article in the "The Economist" magazine that Ms. Marissa Mayer of Yahoo requires all her employees to work in the office, not from home. She indicates that "Speed and quality are often sacrificed when we work from home." I personally do support her idea. I hold that working in the office is more beneficial. I will explain my reasons below.

To begin with, working in the office makes employees able to focus entirely on their tasks. As we are all aware, most organizations nowadays provide their workers with state-of-the-art facilities for workers to use in the office. Employees can just concentrate on what needs to be done without worrying about the availability of devices, such as photocopiers, or high-speed Internet connection, which might not be accessible at home. When working in the office, I myself do sense that my workplace productivity is high and I am able to deliver a pretty high level of performance.

In addition, working in the office enables me, a sales representative, to get involved in discussions more easily. Team members need to participate in meetings from time to time to exchange creative ideas. Although, thanks to advanced technologies, people working at home can also use some sort of video-conferencing equipment to hold meetings, I still prefer to talk to colleagues, partners, or even clients face to face. According to my experience, I have realized that most business deals are made when decision makers are socializing on the golf course, rather than on the Internet. Therefore, I believe face-to-face interaction is more powerful than communication via machines.

Some people might argue that working at home using computers gives workers more freedom, since no one breathes down their necks. This might be true, but I think it requires a huge amount of self-discipline to work alone at home without outside pressure. People working at home might miss out on valuable opportunities to be involved in new or interesting projects.

In conclusion, I think working in the office is better than working at home alone. I personally perform better in a productive working environment, and I also enjoy interacting with people face to face. Working at home might not be a brilliant idea for people who are not self-motivated enough. (378 words)

問題：你喜歡在家利用電腦與電話工作，還是喜歡在辦公室工作？

我日前剛好讀到 "經濟學人" 雜誌中的文章，在討論 Yahoo! 的 Marissa Mayer 小姐要求他所有的員工在辦公室工作而不是家中工作。她指出 "當我們在家工作，時常犧牲掉速度與品質"。我個人確實支持她的想法。我認為在辦公室工作有更多好處。我將於下說明我的理由。

首先，在辦公室工作讓員工能夠完全專注在其任務上。因為我們都知道，現今大多數的企業都提供員工先進的設施，讓員工能在辦公室使用。員工可以只專注在須完成的工作上，而無須顧慮設備的可取用性，像是影印機、或是高速網路連線，這些都是家中可能沒有的。在辦公室工作時，我自己確實感覺到我在工作場所的生產力比較高，而且我可以有更高的績效水準。

此外，在辦公室工作讓身為銷售代表的我能更輕易地投入討論中。團隊成員不時會需要參加會議以交換創意。雖然幸好有先進的技術，在家工作的人也可以用某種視頻會議設備來進行會議，但我仍偏好面對面地跟同事、夥伴或甚至是客戶討論意見。根據我的經驗，我發現大多數的交易都是決策者在高爾夫球場上社交時完成的，而非在網路上。因此，我認為面對面的互動比透過機器溝通更有力。

有些人可能會認為使用電腦在家工作讓員工有更多的自由，因為沒有人在旁緊迫盯人。這可能是真的，但我認為在沒有外在壓力時，獨自在家工作需要很大的自律能力。在家工作的人可能會錯過了參加新奇或有趣專案的寶貴經驗。

總而言之，我認為在辦公室工作比在家獨自工作更好。我個人在較具生產力的辦公環境中表現更好，而且我也很享受與人們面對面的互動。對於沒有足夠自我激勵的人，在家工作可能不是個明智的想法。

文章結構分析

開場段落	I happened to read in an article in the "The Economist" magazine that Ms. Marissa Mayer of Yahoo requires all her employees to work in the office, not from home. She indicates that "Speed and quality are often sacrificed when we work from home." I personally do support her idea. I hold that working in the office is more beneficial. I will explain my reasons below.	說明、引題 ← ← 表態
文章主體 Idea 1	To begin with, working in the office makes employees able to focus entirely on their tasks. As we are all aware, most organizations nowadays provide their workers with state-of-the-art facilities for workers to use in the office. Employees can just concentrate on what needs to be done without worrying about the availability of devices, such as photocopiers, or high-speed Internet connection, which might not be accessible at home. When working in the office, I myself do sense that my workplace productivity is high and I am able to deliver a pretty high level of performance.	主題句 1 ← 細節例證
文章主體 Idea 2	In addition, working in the office enables me, a sales representative, to get involved in discussions more easily. Team members need to participate in meetings from time to time to exchange creative ideas. Although, thanks to advanced technologies, people working at home can also use some sort of video-conferencing equipment to hold meetings, I still prefer to talk to colleagues, partners, or even clients face to face. According to my experience, I have realized that most business deals are made when decision makers are socializing on the golf course, rather than on the Internet. Therefore, I believe face-to-face interaction is more powerful than communication via machines.	主題句 2 ← 細節例證
文章主體 Idea 3	Some people might argue that working at home using computers gives workers more freedom, since no one breathes down their necks. This might be true, but I think it requires a huge amount of self-discipline to work alone at home without outside pressure. People working at home might miss out on valuable opportunities to be involved in new or interesting projects.	反面論述 ← 扭轉意見
結論段落	In conclusion, I think working in the office is better than working at home alone. I personally perform better in a productive working environment, and I also enjoy interacting with people face to face. Working at home might not be a brilliant idea for people who are not self-motivated enough.	重述主要論點

點子發想有方向

因為文化背景，教育體制，與人文性格等種種差異，造成東西方學生在思考能力上的差異。

筆者先舉個真實的例子。筆者曾經與一位資深加拿大外師，一同觀摩台灣老師的兒童美語課程。台灣老師請兩位大約八、九歲的小朋友上台，並問道 Do you like flowers? 的題目，要求兩位小朋友各自在黑板兩邊寫出自己的答案。A 小朋友寫下：I like red flowers and tall. 而 B 小朋友寫的是：I like red flowers.。

想當然爾，老師隨即在 B 小朋友所寫的 I like red flowers. 毫無錯誤的句子上打了個大勾，並標 100 分！並在 A 小朋友所寫的 and tall 兩個字上用紅筆畫了個超級大叉，並標上 50 分！

台灣老師的批改：

A: I like red flowers. and ✗tall.

B: I like red flowers. ✓

看到此時，同學可能不覺得有什麼問題，「這兩句明明就 B 寫得對呀，A 寫的句子有文法錯誤。」是這樣，沒錯吧？！但事後，與加拿大外師討論觀摩感想，他的意見讓筆者有了不同角度的思考。

他說，同樣的兩個句子，A 小朋友所寫的 I like red flowers and tall. 句子，在美國／加拿大的老師眼中看來，有可能得到 A-。而 B 小朋友所寫的文法正確句子 I like red flowers. 可能僅得到 B。為什麼會有這種差異呢？有錯誤的句子分數反而高？！

原因是在於，西方教育重視的並非要得到「標準答案」，他們想訓練的是學習者的「勇於嘗試，不怕犯錯，自由表達」的那種 I'm not sure, but I'm willing to TRY.（我不確定，但願意一試。）的精神。因此，即便 A 句子錯誤，但從中可感受到 A 小朋友試著想要使用更多可以描述花的形容詞的那種努力感 (effort)，西方老師反而會認為這種努力值得嘉許，值得得到一個 A-，以鼓勵這種願意努力一試，從錯誤中學習的人。而 B 句雖說是沒錯，但僅是很「安全」的答案，看不出有新意或有試著使用其他形容詞的努力。

外國老師的批改：

A: I like red flowers and tall. A⁻

B: I like red flowers. B

相反的，絕大多數台灣同學，從小到大經歷過無數次被父母或老師逼著，為了考試，要求分數，且要與同學比高低的經驗，這樣折騰十年下來，本著「要寫標準答案才有分」的宗旨的結果就是，只會背書填空，回答些刁鑽的文法題目，卻完全失去舉一反三，思考活用的能力，更別說會相信「天底下事情是沒有標準答案的」這樣的事了，導致思考僵化，只等別人給答案的窘境。筆者在教學期間最常遇到同學的反應是「我知道要寫五段式作文，三個論點，但看到題目腦筋一片空白，就是想不出來點子呀！」為何會這樣，答案就很明顯了。

❶ 訓練思考能力

那麼，要如何從頭訓練以改善這種「無法思考」的症頭呢?! 首先，請同學一定要有「標準答案是不存在的」這樣的認知，針對一個議題，可以從不同角度思考，從不同層面去看就會有不同答案，英文中有一個片語 think out of the box 不就是這樣的意思嗎？台灣同學的思考能力長期被困在「框框」內了，現在就開始，跳開原有看事情的角度，學外國小朋友一般，天馬行空，自由想像，無關對錯，有錯就改，更不要期待有人會給你標準答案。

再者，要培養獨立思考的能力，就要隨時對事情保有好奇心，比方說看到一則新聞，不要馬上人云亦云，而是可以試著思考：這新聞當事人是誰？他當時真的是這樣講的嗎？有沒有他的話被斷章取義的可能？事件背後原因為何？有沒有證據？事後是否有明確的解決方案？等。也就是說，要從日常生活中的點滴中培養批判思考的能力。

雖說要徹底扭轉僵化的思考，主要應是由個人在日常生活中的思考練習來漸漸達成，筆者還是會列出以下幾種訓練思考的方式給大家參考。但需要再度重申的是，批判思考與解決問題的能力，「絕對不可能」是看了一本書，參考幾個圖表之後，睡一覺起來隔天就突然會了的！若有抱著「買了書，參考了例子就應該要會思考」的讀者，可能要失望了！（書中解釋的五題會了，遇到第六題又不會，那你說該怎麼辦？！）要瞭解，訓練思考邏輯要靠每人從日常生活著手，針對不同議題一次又一次地練習分析，思考，判斷，歸納……等，才有可能期待在有朝一日，培養出自己專屬的思考模式，而不再人云亦云被別人牽著鼻子走。

因此，筆者建議大家，除了參考書的內容之外，平時更應多「做白日夢」，發揮想像力，天馬行空不受限地想奇異的點子。更可以去百貨公司公司坐上一天，觀察人群，他們是誰？他們都買些什麼？什麼產品實用又受歡迎？等。從日常生活中的小思考著手，若考試被問及類似像「你對博愛座的看法」的日常題目時，在平日所準備的點子便可以立即派上用場了！

❷ 優缺點對比的範例

此種思考方式，便是直接將某一議題的「正／反」兩面列出，加以比較優缺點。

Question#1: Should students be required to wear uniforms to school?

Yes	No
One of students' obligations is studying instead of spending time on appearance.	Students wearing uniforms are stuck and won't be able to express themselves.
The uniform is a feature of a school.	Students generally think wearing uniforms is uncomfortable.
Uniforms discourage discriminations between students about their apparel and style.	People naturally have different tastes, and it's pointless to force them to wear exactly the same thing.
Wearing uniform allows students to save time on deciding what to wear.	It's possible to kill students' creativity.
Prepare students for future dress-code rules in the workplace.	Some uniforms are ugly in styles and colors, so students won't feel happy wearing them.

Question#2: For educational purposes, is watching television better than reading books?

Yes	No
Watching television helps make audience understand better with the images and the sound.	A person reading five books could learn from various authors with different opinions, while watching a television program, the audience is learning from one source.
After watching an educational program, I pick up new vocab words and learn new facts.	Reading books helps readers stimulate imagination and increase critical thinking ability.
Watching television is beneficial for people who prefer audio or visual ways of learning.	Books cause human mind to consume new words and sentence structures, and reading engages different parts of the brain.
Television programs are easily available online with the help of modern technology, while finding a book in a library is relatively troublesome.	Reading books helps readers boost creativity, exercise judgement and explore their imagination.

❸ 發展心智圖 (Mind Mapping)

　　此種 mind mapping 思考方式，是將議題相關的元素都列出，可以想到多少就列多少，還可再細分到第二層或第三層去，以更深層地激發腦力。

Question#1: What some advantages and disadvantages of using the Internet?

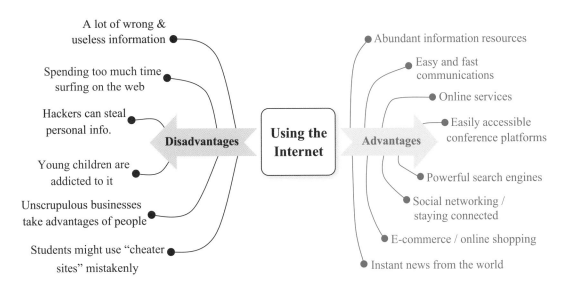

Question#2: What are some factors that contribute to a successful life?

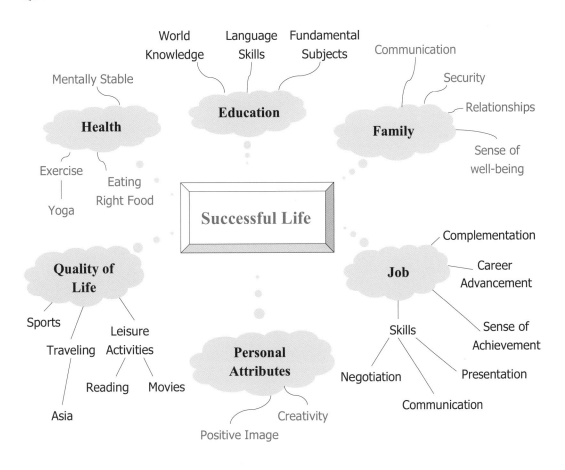

此思考方式也很常用，特性是不用受任何框架的限制，可天馬行空地列出腦中所有的點子。思考時可先不用依照分類、副主題等限制，待將所有可能點子都列出之後，再分類整理即可。列點子方式可依以下 Q1 一般寫下關鍵字，或與他人集思廣益依 Q2 一樣每人列出自己的想法。

Question#1: What are some good ways for people to stay healthy?

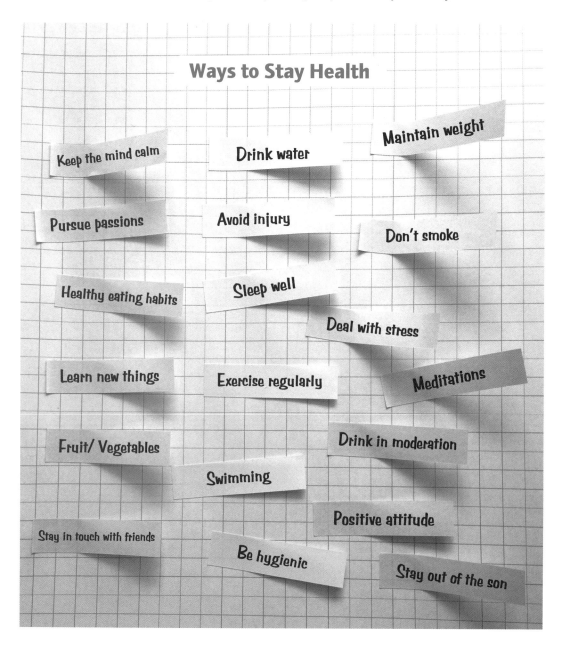

Question#2: What are some strategies that companies use to increase their sales?

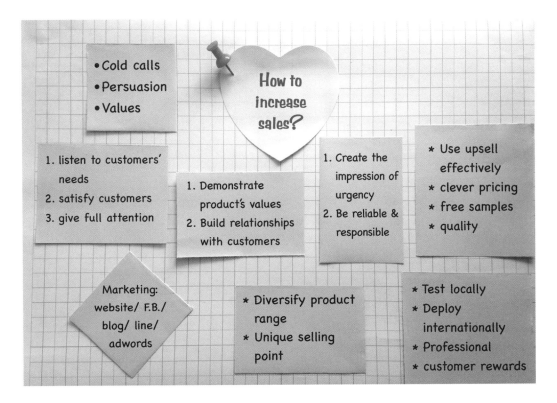

❺ 角度切入 (Perspectives)

　　針對某議題要發表自己的看法,可試著用「不同角度切入」的方式來思考。這些「角度」可以是:從 money(費用)、environment(環保)、safety(安全性)、health(健康)、lifestyle(生活)……等方面來看。這種方式讓思考者有切入的方向可依循,想點子時不致於會發散得太廣,適合時間較緊迫的情境使用。

Question#1: A factory is about to be built in your neighborhood. Discuss some disadvantages of it.

Perspective	Idea
Environment	Emissions from the factory pollute water and land and they can spread far and wide beyond the factory.
Safety	High crime rates are often associated with industrial zones.

Lifestyle	The factory using various equipment are very likely to producing large amount of noise, thus decreases the standard of living in the neighborhood.

Question#2: If you could invent something new, what would it be?

Thesis Statement: I always wanted to invent a "floating vehicle".

Perspective	Idea
Money	The floating vehicle doesn't rely on petroleum, so people using it can save money on fuel.
Environment	The floating vehicle runs cleaner and cuts fuel consumption, thus conserves energy.
Safety	Driving such a floating vehicle is much safer than driving a car, since it can reduce the risk of collision.

6 星展圖 (Star-bursting)

此 Star-bursting 思考方式，如同其名稱一般，便是像星星一般有五個角度發散出去。而此五個角度也是各有其功能的，但跟「角度切入」不同的是，此五個角度分別是 who（人），why（事），when（時），where（地），what（物），與 how（如何）等組成的。也就是說，針對某議題，最直接討論其相關的「5W+1H」要素即可。這樣的思考方式的優點是有直接的焦點，且可節省時間。

另外，雖說其名稱爲「星展圖」，也不代表一定就非要畫星星不可。如同下列 Q2 所示，針對一個置中的主題，可以在外圍構思「5W+1H」的點子便利貼亦可。也不代表只能畫五個角度，若有需要的話，構思六個、七個……角度也是可以的，完全應依個人的彈性需求而定。

Question#1: Your company is about to design a new-generation phone. What factors should the company consider before starting a design?

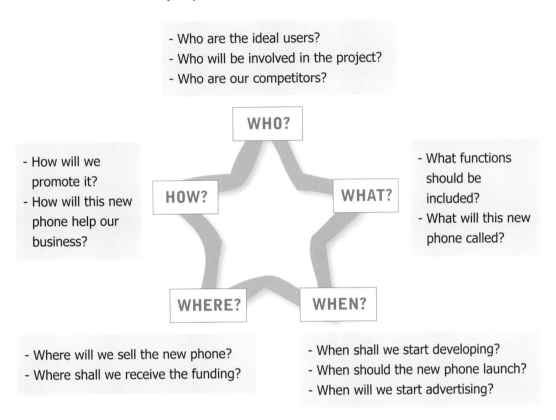

- Who are the ideal users?
- Who will be involved in the project?
- Who are our competitors?

WHO?

- What functions should be included?
- What will this new phone called?

WHAT?

- How will we promote it?
- How will this new phone help our business?

HOW?

WHERE?

- Where will we sell the new phone?
- Where shall we receive the funding?

WHEN?

- When shall we start developing?
- When should the new phone launch?
- When will we start advertising?

Question#2: Desribe a person you admire the most?

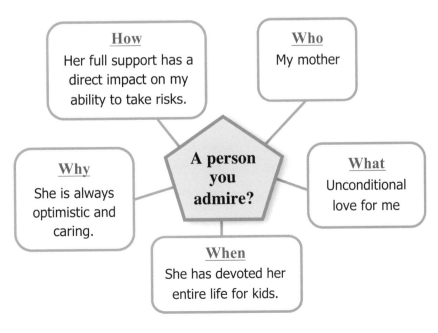

How
Her full support has a direct impact on my ability to take risks.

Who
My mother

Why
She is always optimistic and caring.

A person you admire?

What
Unconditional love for me

When
She has devoted her entire life for kids.

如同前面篇章提過的，要培養英文寫作能力，單字運用能力，甚至於批判思考能力，絕不會是想靠吃下一顆仙丹，或使用什麼魔法英語學習術，或想單靠看一本寫作書就可以養成的。而是要在日常生活當中，不斷地接觸與使用英文，收集資料，參考別人的意見，閱讀議題分析的文章……等，以便讓自己在今後寫作時，有判斷能力進而想出自己的意見，有分析能力可以探討一個議題的正反利弊，與有徹底運用單字確切精準地傳達看法。

在現今網路發達的環境下，可以參考的資料多到簡直無法計數，即便有心想好好找學習資訊的同學，也可能就被淹沒在大量的網站中，而無法判斷哪些是真正實用的資訊了。有鑑於此，筆者將適合同學針對精進寫作，熟悉文法用字，與瞭解時事議題… 等可參考的五十個網站，依八大分類整理出來。方便同學日常就可以參考，收集資料，以增進自身的英文實力。

❶ 線上資源（8 大類，共 50 個資源網）

A. 大學寫作資源中心類：

很多美國大學網站內都設有 Writing Center（寫作中心）的連結，內容包括單字拓展，文法解釋與句型結構等教學。有些甚至將內容整理成 PDF 檔，方便同學下載。

1. The Purdue Online Lab:
   https://owl.english.purdue.edu/

2. Monash University:
   http://www.monash.edu.au/lls/llonline/writing/index.xml

3. Harvard College Writing Center:
   http://writingcenter.fas.harvard.edu/pages/strategies-essay-writing

4. ESC Online Writing Center:
   http://www.esc.edu/online-writing-center/resources/

5. Amherst College Writing Center:
   https://www.amherst.edu/academiclife/support/writingcenter/resourcesforwriters

6. Writing@CSU / The Writing Studio:
   http://writing.colostate.edu/index.cfm

7. Literacy Education Online:
   http://leo.stcloudstate.edu/

B. 線上字典類：

網路發達後，同學便捨棄厚重的傳統字典了，而改用可以不限時地都隨時查閱的線上字典。如同稍早提過的，要瞭解一個單字，不是知道其中文意思就好，而是要一併瞭解其同意字、用法、例句……等。而線上字典的好處便是，針對一個單字的各個層面運用都有列出。同學所熟知的 Cambridge 或 Oxford Dictionaries 也都有出線上版本了。

8. Cambridge Dictionaries Online:
   http://dictionary.cambridge.org/

9. Oxford Dictionaries:
   http://www.oxforddictionaries.com/

10. Oxford Learner's Dictionaries:
    http://www.oxfordlearnersdictionaries.com/

11. Merriam-Webster:
    http://www.merriam-webster.com/

12. Online Collocation Dictionary:
    http://oxforddictionary.so8848.com/

C. 單字／文法／寫作教學類：

下列爲常見又實用的基本英文文法與寫作句型教學的網站。

13. English Page:
    http://www.englishpage.com/

14. Writing Persuasive Essays:
    http://www.ereadingworksheets.com/writing/writing-persuasive-essays/

15. Writefix:
    http://www.writefix.com/

16. Time 4 Writing:
    http://www.time4writing.com/free-writing-resources/

17. Guide to Grammar & Writing:
    http://www.ccc.commnet.edu/grammar/

18. Paradigm Online Writing Assistant:
    http://www.powa.org/

19. Nuts and Bolts Guide:
    http://www.nutsandboltsguide.com/nb-home.html

20. Quick and Dirty Tips:
    http://www.quickanddirtytips.com/education/writing

21. Learning Path:
    http://learningpath.org/articles/Online_Creative_Writing_Courses_Offered_Free_by_Top_Universities_and_Educational_Websites.html

D. 名人演講類：

要在寫作時有充實的內容與豐富的實例可以列舉，最佳的方式之一就是多聽名人演講的內容。這些名人演講之所以會流傳久遠，歷久彌新，就是因為其內容字字珠璣，可以帶給人們莫大的啟發。多聽名人的意見看法，更可以充實自己的內在並提升程度。透過「聽」的同時，還可以練習聽力呢！

22. American Rhetoric Top 100 Speeches:
    http://www.americanrhetoric.com/top100speechesall.html

23. Barack Obama Speeches:
    http://www.americanrhetoric.com/barackobamaspeeches.htm

24. Great Speeches Collection:
    http://www.historyplace.com/speeches/previous.htm

25. TED:
    http://www.ted.com

E. 媒體英語教學類：

要瞭解時事，讓自己在寫作時有點子可以發揮，平日更應該多看時事的披露。但一般來說同學會認為原文新聞單字多，實在很難理解消化。現在很多專業的媒體網站，也都增加了「英語教學」的內容。當然，會是以新聞為素材，以實際（且經過簡化）的新聞時事內容來讓同學學習英文。

26. BBC Learning English:
    http://www.bbc.co.uk/learningenglish/

27. BBC Newsround:
    http://www.bbc.co.uk/newsround

28. CNN Student News:
    http://edition.cnn.com/studentnews

29. VOA Learning English:
    http://learningenglish.voanews.com/

30. The New York Times / The Learning Network:
    http://learning.blogs.nytimes.com/

31. TIME for Kids:
    http://www.timeforkids.com/

32. Student News Net:
    https://www.studentnewsnet.com/

F. 世界知識類：

平日在意見的收集與知識的增進上，應多方涉獵。比方說下列的地理資訊、世界遺產與文學小說方面，也是可以整體提升個人程度的有趣素材。

33. National Geographic:
    http://news.nationalgeographic.com/

34. World Heritage:
    http://whc.unesco.org/

35. Loyal Books:
    http://www.loyalbooks.com

G. 意見收集類：

很多議題都不會是只有單方面的看法，通常會有正反兩面的利與弊觀點。筆者平日最喜歡參考，並可藉此看到不同意見（有時候反方的點子更有道理，但自己卻沒想到！）的網站，便是下列 debate（辯論）類的網站了。這類的網站就是可以讓使用者針對一個議題各自提出正反兩面的看法。比方說議題是：學生是否應該穿制服？那麼網站上就會有不同背景的人留言，支持要穿制服的人會列出穿制服的好處，認爲應該

不要穿制服的人也會提出理由。同時可以看到不同角度的意見的好處是，訓練自己的思考不再是單方向的，也可以從中學習批判思考的能力喔！

36. Debate: http://www.debate.org/

37. IDEA (International Debate Education Association): http://idebate.org/

38. Create Debate: http://www.createdebate.com/

39. ProCon: http://www.procon.org/debate-topics.php

40. Debating Europe: http://www.debatingeurope.eu/

H. 議題分析類：

最後，這類議題分析類的網站內容，不單單是像新聞一樣將事件報導出來就好。而是還會加入評論，分析前因後果、未來影響……等意見。除了瞭解別人看事情的角度之外，更可以藉由閱讀這些英文文章當中，學習到句型與單字應用喔！

41. American Thinker: http://www.americanthinker.com/

42. National Review: http://www.nationalreview.com/

43. The Washington Free Beacon: http://freebeacon.com/

44. PJ Media: https://pjmedia.com/

45. How Stuff Works: http://www.howstuffworks.com/

46. TIME: http://time.com

47. Inc.: http://www.inc.com

48. Success: http://www.success.com

49. Social Media Today: http://www.socialmediatoday.com/

50. Info Please: http://www.infoplease.com/world.html

1 Type – Agree or Disagree

1. Do you agree or disagree with the following statement? People are never satisfied with what they have; they always want something more or something different. Use specific reasons or examples to support your answer.

2. Do you agree or disagree with the following statement? There is nothing that young people can teach older people.

3. Do you agree or disagree with the following statement? A person's childhood years (the time from birth to twelve years of age) are the most important years of a person's life.

4. Do you agree or disagree with the following statement? Children should be required to help with household tasks as soon as they are able to do so.

5. Do you agree or disagree with the following statement? People behave differently when they wear different clothes. Do you agree that different clothes influence the way people behave?

6. It is better for children to grow up in the countryside than in a big city. Do you agree or disagree?

7. Do you agree or disagree with the following statement? People should sometimes do things that they do not enjoy doing.

8. The expression "Never, never give up" means to keep trying and never stop working for your goals. Do you agree or disagree with this statement?

9. Do you agree or disagree with the following statement? One should never judge a person by external appearances.

10. Do you agree or disagree with the following statement? Parents or other adult relatives should make important decisions for their older (15 to 18 year-old) teenage children.

11. Do you agree or disagree with the following statement? Playing games teaches us about life.

12. Do you agree or disagree with the following statement? A zoo has no useful purpose.

13. It is sometimes said that borrowing money from a friend can harm or damage the friendship. Do you agree? Why or why not?

14. Do you agree or disagree with the following statement? People should read only those books that are about real events, real people, and established facts.

15. Do you agree or disagree with the following statement? It is more important for students to study history and literature than it is for them to study science and mathematics.

16. Do you agree or disagree with the following statement? All students should be required to study art and music in secondary school.

17. Do you agree or disagree with the following statement? High schools should allow students to study the courses that students want to study.

18. Do you agree or disagree with the following statement? Parents are the best teachers.

19. Schools should ask students to evaluate their teachers. Do you agree or disagree?

20. Do you agree or disagree that progress is always good?

21. Do you agree or disagree with the following statement? With the help of technology, students nowadays can learn more information and learn it more quickly.

22. Do you agree or disagree with the following statement? Most experiences in our lives that seemed difficult at the time become valuable lessons for the future.

23. Do you agree or disagree with the following statement? Classmates are a more important influence than parents on a child's success in school.

24. Do you agree or disagree with the following statement? Children should begin learning a foreign language as soon as they start school.

25. Do you agree or disagree with the following statement? Boys and girls should attend separate schools.

26. Do you agree or disagree with the following statement? Teachers should be paid according to how much their students learn.

27. Do you agree or disagree with the following statement? Reading fiction (such as novels and short stories) is more enjoyable than watching movies.

28. Do you agree or disagree with the following statement? Playing a game is fun only when you win.

29. Do you agree or disagree with the following statement? Attending a live performance (for example, a play, concert, or sporting event) is more enjoyable than watching the same event on television.

30. Do you agree or disagree with the following statement? Games are as important for adults as they are for children.

31. Do you agree or disagree with the following statement? Dancing plays an important role in a culture.

32. Do you agree or disagree with the following statement? Watching television is bad for children.

33. Do you agree or disagree with the following statement? Only people who earn a lot of money are successful.

34. Decisions can be made quickly, or they can be made after careful thought. Do you agree or disagree with the following statement? The decisions that people make quickly are always wrong.

35. "When people succeed, it is because of hard work. Luck has nothing to do with success." Do you agree or disagree with the quotation above?

36. Businesses should hire employees for their entire lives. Do you agree or disagree?

37. Do you agree or disagree with the following statement? Face-to-face communication is better than other types of communication, such as letters, email, or telephone calls.

38. Do you agree or disagree with the following statement? The most important aspect of a job is the money a person earns.

39. Do you agree or disagree with the following statement? A person should never make an important decision alone.

40. Do you agree or disagree with the following statement? It is better to be a member of a group than to be the leader of a group.

41. Do you agree or disagree with the following statement? Technology has made the world a better place to live.

42. Do you agree or disagree with the following statement? Modern technology is creating a single world culture.

43. Do you agree or disagree with the following statement? Telephones and email have made communication between people less personal.

44. Do you agree or disagree with the following statement? Television, newspapers, magazines, and other media pay too much attention to the personal lives of famous people such as public figures and celebrities.

45. Learning about the past has no value for those of us living in the present. Do you agree or disagree?

46. Do you agree or disagree with the following statement? Advertising can tell you a lot about a country.

47. Some young children spend a great amount of their time practicing sports. Discuss the advantages and disadvantages of this.

48. Do you agree or disagree with the following statement? Universities should give the same amount of money to their students' sports activities as they give to their university libraries.

49. Do you agree or disagree with the following statement? The best way to travel is in a group led by a tour guide.

2 Type – Choice / Preference

50. What do you consider to be the most important room in a house? Why is this room more important to you than any other room?

51. Some items (such as clothes or furniture) can be made by hand or by machine. Which do you prefer — items made by hand or items made by machine?

52. A gift (such as a camera, a soccer ball, or an animal) can contribute to a child's development. What gift would you give to help a child develop? Why?

53. Some people choose friends who are different from themselves. Others choose friends who are similar to themselves. Compare the advantages of having friends who are different from you with the advantages of having friends who are similar to you. Which kind of friend do you prefer for yourself? Why?

54. Some people enjoy change, and they look forward to new experiences. Others like their lives to stay the same, and they do not change their usual habits. Compare these two approaches to life.

55. Some people think that the family is the most important influence on young adults. Other people think that friends are the most important influence on young adults. Which view do you agree with?

56. Some people like doing work by hand. Others prefer using machines. Which do you prefer?

57. Groups or organizations are an important part of some people's lives. Why are groups or organizations important to people?

58. What are some of the qualities of a good parent?

59. You have been told that dormitory rooms at your university must be shared by two students. Would you rather have the university assign a student to share a room with you, or would you rather choose your own roommate?

60. Some people prefer to live in places that have the same weather or climate all year long. Others like to live in areas where the weather changes several times a year. Which do you prefer?

61. Some people prefer to eat at food stands or restaurants. Other people prefer to prepare and eat food at home. Which do you prefer?

62. Some people believe that the Earth is being harmed (damaged) by human activity. Others feel that human activity makes the Earth a better place to live. What is your opinion?

63. Some people spend their entire lives in one place. Others move a number of times throughout their lives, looking for a better job, house, community, or even climate. Which do you prefer: staying in one place or moving in search of another place?

64. Is it better to enjoy your money when you earn it or is it better to save your money for some time in the future?

65. Some people prefer to get up early in the morning and start the day's work. Others prefer to get up later in the day and work until late at night. Which do you prefer?

66. Some people are always in a hurry to go places and get things done. Other people prefer to take their time and live life at a slower pace. Which do you prefer?

67. Some people prefer to spend most of their time alone. Others like to be with friends most of the time. Do you prefer to spend your time alone or with friends?

68. Would you prefer to live in a traditional house or in a modern apartment building? Use specific reasons and details to support your choice.

69. Many parts of the world are losing important natural resources, such as forests, animals, or clean water. Choose one resource that is disappearing and explain why it needs to be saved.

70. People remember special gifts or presents that they have received. Why?

71. People do many different things to stay healthy. What do you do for good health?

72. People recognize a difference between children and adults. What events (experiences or ceremonies) make a person an adult?

73. Some people say that physical exercise should be a required part of every school day. Other people believe that students should spend the whole school day on academic studies. Which opinion do you agree with?

74. Some high schools require all students to wear school uniforms. Other high schools permit students to decide what to wear to school. Which of these two school policies do you think is better?

75. People learn in different ways. Some people learn by doing things; other people learn by reading about things; others learn by listening to people talk about things. Which of these methods of learning is best for you?

76. When students move to a new school, they sometimes face problems. How can schools help these students with their problems?

77. Some students like classes where teachers lecture (do all of the talking) in class. Other students prefer classes where the students do some of the talking. Which type of class do you prefer?

78. Some students prefer to study alone. Others prefer to study with a group of students. Which do you prefer?

79. Some universities require students to take classes in many subjects. Other universities require students to specialize in one subject. Which is better?

80. Some people believe that university students should be required to attend classes. Others believe that going to classes should be optional for students. Which point of view do you agree with?

81. Some people think that they can learn better by themselves than with a teacher. Others think that it is always better to have a teacher. Which do you prefer?

82. Some people like to do only what they already do well. Other people prefer to try new things and take risks. Which do you prefer?

83. Students at universities often have a choice of places to live. They may choose to live in university dormitories, or they may choose to live in apartments in the community. Compare the advantages of living in university housing with the advantages of living in an apartment in the community. Where would you prefer to live?

84. Some people believe that a college or university education should be available to all students. Others believe that higher education should be available only to good students. Discuss these views. Which view do you agree with?

85. Is the ability to read and write more important today than in the past? Why or why not?

86. Your school has enough money to purchase either computers for students or books for the library. Which should your school choose to buy — computers or books?

87. Many students choose to attend schools or universities outside their home countries. Why do some students study abroad?

88. Some people prefer to plan activities for their free time very carefully. Others choose not to make any plans at all for their free time. Compare the benefits of planning free-time activities with the benefits of not making plans. Which do you prefer — planning or not planning for your leisure time?

89. People listen to music for different reasons and at different times. Why is music important to many people?

90. Many people have a close relationship with their pets. These people treat their birds, cats, or other animals as members of their family. In your opinion, are such relationships good? Why or why not?

91. Films can tell us a lot about the country where they were made. What have you learned about a country from watching its movies?

92. You have received a gift of money. The money is enough to buy either a piece of jewelry you like or tickets to a concert you want to attend. Which would you buy?

93. Some movies are serious, designed to make the audience think. Other movies are designed primarily to amuse and

entertain. Which type of movie do you prefer?

94. Some people believe that students should be given one long vacation each year. Others believe that students should have several short vacations throughout the year. Which viewpoint do you agree with?

95. Some people prefer to spend their free time outdoors. Other people prefer to spend their leisure time indoors. Would you prefer to be outside or would you prefer to be inside for your leisure activities?

96. A university plans to develop a new research center in your country. Some people want a center for business research. Other people want a center for research in agriculture (farming). Which of these two kinds of research centers do you recommend for your country?

97. Is it more important to be able to work with a group of people on a team or to work independently?

98. Some people prefer to work for a large company. Others prefer to work for a small company. Which would you prefer?

99. Some people believe that success in life comes from taking risks or chances. Others believe that success results from careful planning. In your opinion, what does success come from?

100. A company is going to give some money either to support the arts or to

protect the environment. Which do you think the company should choose?

101. Some people prefer to work for themselves or own a business. Others prefer to work for an employer. Would you rather be self- employed, work for someone else, or own a business?

102. Which would you choose: a high-paying job with long hours that would give you little time with family and friends or a lower-paying job with shorter hours that would give you more time with family and friends?

103. Some people say that advertising encourages us to buy things we really do not need. Others say that advertisements tell us about new products that may improve our lives. Which viewpoint do you agree with?

104. You have enough money to purchase either a house or a business. Which would you choose to buy?

105. Some famous athletes and entertainers earn millions of dollars every year. Do you think these people deserve such high salaries?

106. When people need to complain about a product or poor service, some prefer to complain in writing and others prefer to complain in person. Which way do you prefer?

107. Some people say that the Internet provides people with a lot of valuable information. Others think access to so much information creates problems.

Which view do you agree with?

108. Choose one of the following transportation vehicles and explain why you think it has changed people's lives: automobiles / bicycles / airplanes

109. Some people think that human needs for farmland, housing, and industry are more important than saving land for endangered animals. Do you agree or disagree with this point of view? Why or why not?

110. Some people think that the automobile has improved modern life. Others think that the automobile has caused serious problems. What is your opinion?

111. Some people say that computers have made life easier and more convenient. Other people say that computers have made life more complex and stressful. What is your opinion?

112. In the future, students may have the choice of studying at home by using technology such as computers or television or of studying at traditional schools. Which would you prefer?

113. Some people think that governments should spend as much money as possible on developing or buying computer technology. Other people disagree and think that this money should be spent on more basic needs. Which one of these opinions do you agree with?

114. Every generation of people is different in important ways. How is your generation different from your parents' generation?

115. The 21st century has begun. What changes do you think this new century will bring?

116. In your country, is there more need for land to be left in its natural condition or is there more need for land to be developed for housing and industry?

117. Some people prefer to live in a small town. Others prefer to live in a big city. Which place would you prefer to live in?

118. Some people think governments should spend as much money as possible exploring outer space (for example, traveling to the Moon and to other planets). Other people disagree and think governments should spend this money for our basic needs on Earth. Which of these two opinions do you agree with?

119. Your school has received a gift of money. What do you think is the best way for your school to spend this money?

120. What is the most important animal in your country? Why is the animal important?

121. In some countries, people are no longer allowed to smoke in many public places and office buildings. Do you think this is a good rule or a bad rule?

122. Plants can provide food, shelter, clothing, or medicine. What is one kind of plant that is important to you or the people in your country?

123. When famous people such as actors, athletes and rock stars give their opinions, many people listen. Do you think we should pay attention to these opinions?

124. The twentieth century saw great change. In your opinion, what is one change that should be remembered about the twentieth century?

125. You have decided to give several hours of your time each month to improve the community where you live. What is one thing you will do to improve your community? Why?

126. Imagine that you are preparing for a trip. You plan to be away from your home for a year. In addition to clothing and personal care items, you can take one additional thing. What would you take and why?

127. Some people like to travel with a companion. Other people prefer to travel alone. Which do you prefer?

3 Type– Description

128. In your opinion, what is the most important characteristic (for example, honesty, intelligence, a sense of humor) that a person can have to be successful in life?

129. If you were asked to send one thing representing your country to an international exhibition, what would you choose? Why?

130. Your city has decided to build a statue or monument to honor a famous person in your country. Who would you choose?

131. Describe a custom from your country that you would like people from other countries to adopt.

132. A foreign visitor has only one day to spend in your country. Where should this visitor go on that day? Why?

133. If you could go back to some time and place in the past, when and where would you go? Why?

134. What discovery in the last 100 years has been most beneficial for people in your country?

135. Many students have to live with roommates while going to school or university. What are some of the important qualities of a good roommate?

136. People have different ways of escaping the stress and difficulties of modern life. Some read; some exercise; others work in their gardens. What do you think are the best ways of reducing stress?

137. People attend college or university for many different reasons (for example, new experiences, career preparation, increased knowledge). Why do you think people attend college or university?

138. Nowadays, food has become easier to prepare. Has this change improved the way people live?

139. A company has announced that it wishes to build a large factory near your community. Discuss the advantages and disadvantages of this new influence on your community. Do you support or oppose the factory?

140. It has recently been announced that a new restaurant may be built in your neighborhood. Do you support or oppose this plan? Why?

141. It has recently been announced that a new movie theater may be built in your neighborhood. Do you support or oppose this plan? Why?

142. It has recently been announced that a new high school may be built in your community. Do you support or oppose this plan? Why?

143. What is a very important skill a person should learn in order to be successful in the world today?

144. It has recently been announced that a large shopping center may be built in your neighborhood. Do you support or oppose this plan? Why?

145. Why do you think some people are attracted to dangerous sports or other dangerous activities?

146. How do movies or television influence people's behavior?

147. Many people visit museums when they travel to new places. Why do you think people visit museums?

148. Should governments spend more money on improving roads and highways, or should governments spend more money on improving public transportation (buses, trains, subways)? Why?

149. In general, people are living longer now. Discuss the causes of this phenomenon.

150. In some countries, teenagers have jobs while they are still students. Do you think this is a good idea?

151. A person you know is planning to move to your town or city. What do you think this person would like and dislike about living in your town or city? Why?

152. Neighbors are the people who live near us. In your opinion, what are the qualities of a good neighbor?

153. What are the important qualities of a good son or daughter? Have these qualities changed or remained the same over time in your culture?

154. What are some important qualities of a good supervisor (boss)?

155. We all work or will work in our jobs with many different kinds of people. In your opinion, what are some important characteristics of a co-worker (someone you work closely with)?

156. People work because they need money to live. What are some other reasons that people work?

157. What change would make your hometown more appealing to people your age?

158. What do you want most in a friend — someone who is intelligent, or someone who has a sense of humor, or someone who is reliable? Which one of these characteristics is most important to you?

159. Should a city try to preserve its old, historic buildings or destroy them and replace them with modern buildings?

160. Many teachers assign homework to students every day. Do you think that daily homework is necessary for students?

4 Type– If / What (What will you do in a certain scenario?)

161. If you could invent something new, what product would you develop?

162. Imagine that you have received some land to use as you wish. How would you use this land?

163. You have the opportunity to visit a foreign country for two weeks. Which country would you like to visit?

164. If you could make one important change in a school that you attended, what change would you make?

165. If you could change one important

thing about your hometown, what would you change?

166. If you were an employer, which kind of worker would you prefer to hire: an inexperienced worker at a lower salary or an experienced worker at a higher salary?

167. If you could study a subject that you have never had the opportunity to study, what would you choose?

168. If you could travel back in time to meet a famous person from history, what person would you like to meet?

169. If you could meet a famous entertainer or athlete, who would that be, and why?

170. If you could ask a famous person one question, what would you ask? Why?

171. Holidays honor people or events. If you could create a new holiday, what person or event would it honor and how would you want people to celebrate it?

5 Type – Compare and Contrast

172. It has been said, "Not everything that is learned is contained in books." Compare and contrast knowledge gained from experience with knowledge gained from books. In your opinion, which source is more important? Why?

173. When people move to another country, some of them decide to follow the customs of the new country. Others

prefer to keep their own customs. Compare these two choices. Which one do you prefer?

174. Some people trust their first impressions about a person's character because they believe these judgments are generally correct. Other people do not judge a person's character quickly because they believe first impressions are often wrong. Compare these two attitudes. Which attitude do you agree with?

175. Some young children spend a great amount of their time practicing sports. Discuss the advantages and disadvantages of this.

176. A friend of yours has received some money and plans to use all of it either to go on vacation or to buy a car. Your friend has asked you for advice.

Compare your friend's two choices and explain which one you think your friend should choose.

177. Movies are popular all over the world. Explain why movies are so popular.

178. Some people believe that the best way of learning about life is by listening to the advice of family and friends. Other people believe that the best way of learning about life is through personal experience. Compare the advantages of these two different ways of learning about life. Which do you think is preferable?

179. You need to travel from your home to a place 40 miles (64 kilometers) away. Compare the different kinds of transportation you could use. Tell which method of travel you would choose.

1 Type#1 – Career

1. Businesses should hire employees for their entire lives. Do you agree or disagree?

2. Some people prefer to work for a large company. Others prefer to work for a small company. Which would you prefer?

3. Do you agree or disagree that progress is always good?

4. Some people enjoy change, and they look forward to new experiences. Others like their lives to stay the same, and they do not change their usual habits. Compare these two approaches to life.

5. Some people like to do only what they already do well. Other people prefer to try new things and take risks. Which do you prefer?

6. Some people prefer to work for themselves or own a business. Others prefer to work for an employer. Would you rather be self-employed, work for someone else, or own a business?

7. What are some important qualities of a good supervisor (boss)?

8. If you were an employer, which kind of worker would you prefer to hire: an inexperienced worker at a lower salary or an experienced worker at a higher salary?

9. Which would you choose: a high-paying job with long hours that would give you little time with family and friends or a lower-paying job with shorter hours that would give you more time with family and friends?

2 Type#2 – Communication

10. When people need to complain about a product or poor service, some prefer to complain in writing and others prefer to complain in person. Which way do you prefer?

11. Do you agree or disagree with the following statement? Face-to-face communication is better than other types of communication, such as letters, email, or telephone calls.

12. Do you agree or disagree with the following statement? There is nothing that young people can teach older people.

13. Do you agree or disagree with the following statement? People behave differently when they wear different clothes. Do you agree that different clothes influence the way people behave?

14. Do you agree or disagree with the following statement? One should never judge a person by external appearances.

15. Do you agree or disagree with the following statement? People should read only those books that are about real events, real people, and established facts.

16. Do you agree or disagree with the following statement? Advertising can tell you a lot about a country.

17. Some people trust their first impressions about a person's character because they believe these judgments are generally correct. Other people do not judge a person's character quickly because they believe first impressions are often wrong. Compare these two attitudes. Which attitude do you agree with?

3 Type#3 – Decision Making

18. Decisions can be made quickly, or they can be made after careful thought. Do you agree or disagree with the following statement? The decisions that people make quickly are always wrong.

19. Do you agree or disagree with the following statement? A person should never make an important decision alone.

20. Do you agree or disagree with the following statement? People should sometimes do things that they do not enjoy doing.

21. Would you prefer to live in a traditional house or in a modern apartment building? Use specific reasons and details to support your choice.

22. A company has announced that it wishes to build a large factory near your community. Discuss the advantages and disadvantages of this new influence on your community. Do you support or oppose the factory?

23. Some people say that advertising encourages us to buy things we really do not need. Others say that advertisements tell us about new products that may improve our lives. Which viewpoint do you agree with?

4 Type#4 – Environment

24. Some people prefer to live in places that have the same weather or climate all year long. Others like to live in areas where the weather changes several times a year. Which do you prefer?

25. Some people believe that the Earth is being harmed (damaged) by human activity. Others feel that human activity makes the Earth a better place to live. What is your opinion?

26. Many parts of the world are losing important natural resources, such as forests, animals, or clean water. Choose one resource that is disappearing and explain why it needs to be saved.

5 Type#5 – Friendship

27. It is sometimes said that borrowing money from a friend can harm or damage the friendship. Do you agree? Why or why not?

28. Some people prefer to spend most of their time alone. Others like to be with friends most of the time. Do you prefer to spend your time alone or with friends?

6 Type#6 – Hi-Tech

29. Do you agree or disagree with the following statement? Technology has made the world a better place to live.

30. Do you agree or disagree with the

following statement? Modern technology is creating a single world culture.

31. Do you agree or disagree with the following statement? Telephones and email have made communication between people less personal.

32. Do you agree or disagree with the following statement? Television, newspapers, magazines, and other media pay too much attention to the personal lives of famous people such as public figures and celebrities.

33. Some people say that the Internet provides people with a lot of valuable information. Others think access to so much information creates problems. Which view do you agree with?

34. Some people say that computers have made life easier and more convenient. Other people say that computers have made life more complex and stressful. What is your opinion?

7 Type#7 – Leisure

35. Do you agree or disagree with the following statement? Attending a live performance (for example, a play, concert, or sporting event) is more enjoyable than watching the same event on television.

36. Do you agree or disagree with the following statement? Dancing plays an important role in a culture.

37. Some people prefer to plan activities for their free time very carefully. Others choose not to make any plans at all for

their free time. Compare the benefits of planning free-time activities with the benefits of not making plans. Which do you prefer — planning or not planning for your leisure time?

38. Some people prefer to spend their free time outdoors. Other people prefer to spend their leisure time indoors. Would you prefer to be outside or would you prefer to be inside for your leisure activities?

8 Type#8 – Lifestyle

39. It is better for children to grow up in the countryside than in a big city. Do you agree or disagree?

40. Some people are always in a hurry to go places and get things done. Other people prefer to take their time and live life at a slower pace. Which do you prefer?

41. People do many different things to stay healthy. What do you do for good health?

42. Some people prefer to live in a small town. Others prefer to live in a big city. Which place would you prefer to live in?

43. People have different ways of escaping the stress and difficulties of modern life. Some read; some exercise; others work in their gardens. What do you think are the best ways of reducing stress?

9 Type#9 – Money

44. Do you agree or disagree with the following statement? The most

important aspect of a job is the money a person earns.

45. Is it better to enjoy your money when you earn it or is it better to save your money for some time in the future?

46. A company is going to give some money either to support the arts or to protect the environment. Which do you think the company should choose?

47. Should governments spend more money on improving roads and highways, or should governments spend more money on improving public transportation (buses, trains, subways)? Why?

48. People work because they need money to live. What are some other reasons that people work?

49. You have enough money to purchase either a house or a business. Which would you choose to buy?

50. Some famous athletes and entertainers earn millions of dollars every year. Do you think these people deserve such high salaries?

Type#10 – Success

51. Do you agree or disagree with the following statement? Only people who earn a lot of money are successful.

52. "When people succeed, it is because of hard work. Luck has nothing to do with success." Do you agree or disagree with the quotation above?

53. The expression "Never, never give up" means to keep trying and never stop working for your goals. Do you agree or disagree with this statement?

54. Some people believe that success in life comes from taking risks or chances. Others believe that success results from careful planning. In your opinion, what does success come from?

55. In your opinion, what is the most important characteristic (for example, honesty, intelligence, a sense of humor) that a person can have to be successful in life?

56. What is a very important skill a person should learn in order to be successful in the world today?

Type#11 – Teamwork

57. Is it more important to be able to work with a group of people on a team or to work independently?

58. Do you agree or disagree with the following statement? It is better to be a member of a group than to be the leader of a group.

59. Groups or organizations are an important part of some people's lives. Why are groups or organizations important to people?

60. We all work or will work in our jobs with many different kinds of people. In your opinion, what are some important characteristics of a co-worker (someone you work closely with)?

國家圖書館出版品預行編目(CIP)資料

得心應手寫英文：迎戰高分寫作 / 文喬作；-- 初版.
  -- 臺北市：貝塔，2017.01
    面：　公分
  ISBN: 978-986-92044-9-1（平裝）

  1. 英語　2. 寫作法

805.17　　　　　　　　　　　　　　　105020568

得心應手寫英文：迎戰高分寫作

作　　者／文喬
執行編輯／朱慧瑛

出　　版／波斯納出版有限公司
地　　址／台北市 100 中正區館前路 26 號 6 樓
電　　話／(02) 2314-2525
傳　　真／(02) 2312-3535
郵　　撥／19493777 波斯納出版有限公司
客服專線／(02) 2314-3535
客服信箱／btservice@betamedia.com.tw

總 經 銷／時報文化出版企業股份有限公司
地　　址／桃園市龜山區萬壽路二段 351 號
電　　話／(02) 2306-6842

出版日期／2021 年 1 月初版二刷
定　　價／380 元
Ｉ Ｓ Ｂ Ｎ／978-986-92044-9-1

貝塔網址：www.betamedia.com.tw

喚醒你的英文語感！

Get a Feel for English !

喚醒你的英文語感！

Get a Feel for English !

喚醒你的英文語感！

Get a Feel for English !